Renew online at
www.librarieswest.org.uk
or by phoning any Bristol library
Bristol Libraries

PLEASE RETURN BOOK BY LAST DATE STAMPED

BR100

21055 Print Servicess

D0186342

Also by Emerald Fennell

Shiverton Hall

SHIVERTON HALL

THE CREEPER

EMERALD FENNELL

BLOOMSBURY
LONDON NEW DELHI NEW YORK SYDNEY

Bloomsbury Publishing, London, New Delhi, New York and Sydney

First published in Great Britain in June 2014 by Bloomsbury Publishing Plc
50 Bedford Square, London WC1B 3DP

www.bloomsbury.com

Bloomsbury is a registered trademark of Bloomsbury Publishing Plc

A CIP catalogue record for this book is available from the British Library

ISBN 978 1 4088 2779 6

MIX
Paper from
responsible sources
FSC® C020471

Typeset by Hewer Text UK Ltd, Edinburgh
Printed and bound in Great Britain by CPI Group (UK) Ltd, Croydon CR0 4YY

1 3 5 7 9 10 8 6 4 2

For my family – Mum, Dad, Coco, Chris and Daisy

DO NOT READ THIS BOOK.

The message was scrawled inside the crumbling cover in a shaking hand.

And underneath, in an unpunctuated string of quivering letters:

helpmehelpmepleasehelpmehelpmehelpmehelphelphelpme
pleaseplease
please
please
help me
please
please
help me

1

'What on earth . . . ?' Andrew murmured, turning the small book over in his hands.

It seemed ancient, bound in dry, chapped leather, and the paper within was a sickly yellow. Deep claw marks scarred the front and some of the pages had been torn away as though an animal had been at it.

Andrew looked at the warning in the front again: *DO NOT READ THIS BOOK.*

He glanced around his bedroom anxiously; there was his old teddy, Baba, and his striped wallpaper, and the photograph of his family, his mum, his dad and his younger sister, Debbie. All as it had been a few moments before. But the room felt different somehow, colder. His mum usually had the heating up full blast in the winter – much to his father's annoyance – but Andrew felt a draught whispering from some unseen crack, and something else too that he couldn't quite identify.

He laughed a little too loudly, to try to dispel the unease that seemed to have lurched uninvited into his cosy bedroom. His parents had gone to watch Debbie's ballet recital at Grimstone Town Hall. He now regretted begging them to be allowed to stay at home alone for the first time without a babysitter. 'I'm old enough now,' he had whined. 'I'm thirteen.'

It wasn't his only regret of the day.

Andrew should have known that Ronnie was up to something. Earlier that evening they'd been on a bike ride when Ronnie had grinned and said he wanted to take a shortcut home. Andrew started to suspect something as they reached the crumbling gates of Shiverton Hall, which was shut up for the Christmas holidays, but he wanted to impress Ronnie, so he said nothing.

Andrew didn't want to admit it to himself, but the mere mention of Shiverton Hall had made the pulse twitch in his wrists ever since he was a boy. Everyone from Grimstone knew the stories about the place. You'd have to be a nutter to want to go to school there.

'Ronnie,' Andrew called as they pedalled towards the school's enormous, stony silhouette, black against the grey sky. 'What are we doing?'

'You'll see,' Ronnie shouted back and steered his handlebars towards the side of the school, narrowly missing a mossy gargoyle that leaned menacingly out of the wall.

It was growing dark, and not a single light shone out from the vast, turreted heap. Andrew's eyes flickered upwards for a moment, but he could not bear to look at the windows, for fear of what might be peering out of them.

They arrived at the back of the school, by the main quad, with its hideous fountain, where the pointy-toothed mermaid perched, belching brown water from her half-smiling mouth.

'Grotty, isn't she?' Ronnie said, nodding towards the mermaid. 'Grotty' was Ronnie's new favourite word; he'd heard it on some Australian TV show and couldn't stop saying it. Andrew agreed that she was extremely grotty, and then asked what on earth they were doing.

'You're not scared, are you?' Ronnie teased.

'No,' Andrew replied, puffing out his chest. 'It's just it's getting dark and we might get caught.'

'Don't worry, the headmistress is on holiday and the groundsman is in the pub.' He paused and dropped his voice to a spooky whisper. 'We're completely alone.'

'Cut it out!' Andrew said.

'So, do you want to go inside?'

There was a flight of cracked, narrow steps at the base of the school, which led down to a flaky, black cellar door. It stood ajar by a crack.

'I'm not sure about this,' Andrew whispered.

'Don't worry,' Ronnie answered. 'I brought a couple of torches.'

Andrew couldn't think of a response to this, so he meekly accepted.

'You go first,' Ronnie said, giving Andrew a little push towards the door.

'All right!' Andrew shrieked, the panic becoming impossible to disguise. 'I'm going. Don't push me.'

The door creaked open, and Andrew swept the torch around the room, its weak beam catching on the glimmering threads of cobwebs. The cellar looked as though no one had entered it in decades; a few rusting iron bedsteads were piled up in one corner, and decomposing leaves

4

clumped in rotting heaps on the floor, squelched under-foot. An old beer can gleamed among the dust, making Andrew briefly wonder if some poor soul had once lived there. Or maybe the sixth-formers used the old place as a den, he thought, the idea comforting him a little.

Andrew let himself breathe. There was nothing to be frightened of: it was just an empty room.

Then the door shut with a slam behind him and in his alarm he dropped the torch. He could hear Ronnie laughing on the other side. Andrew struggled to yank it open, but the handle was greasy and kept slipping from his grip. 'Please,' Andrew begged. 'Ronnie, please.' Ronnie held the door fast.

Suddenly he felt the door give, and with a cry of relief he pulled it towards him.

'I'm going to kill you!' Andrew said, his voice still shaking.

'Shhhh!' Ronnie replied. He had climbed halfway up the steps and was staring at something across the quad.

'What is it?' Andrew asked reluctantly.

Ronnie turned to him, his finger on his lips, and then beckoned for Andrew to join him. Andrew did so grudgingly.

'Keep your head down,' Ronnie hissed. 'Look!'

Andrew followed his friend's gaze, past the mermaid fountain. It was almost dark, and a thin mist had begun to slither across the grounds.

'I don't see anything,' Andrew whispered.

'Over there,' Ronnie whispered back.

Once Andrew saw it, he immediately regretted looking. A dark figure, hooded and hunched, was creeping along the path away from them; occasionally pausing to check it was alone. The mist and the long, black cloak made it seem as though it was gliding above the ground.

'Let's go,' Andrew said under his breath. 'I don't like it.'

'Where's your sense of adventure?' Ronnie whispered. 'Let's follow it!'

'No, Ronnie, please.' Andrew could hear the whine return to his voice, but he didn't care. 'Let's go home.'

'You can go home,' Ronnie said, tiptoeing up the steps. 'You'd better just hope that thing doesn't catch you on your way back.'

Andrew stood paralysed at the top of the stairs. He didn't want to go with Ronnie, but the idea of cycling alone in the dark seemed equally terrifying.

'Come on,' Ronnie urged. 'It's getting away.'

Andrew took a deep breath and followed his friend.

The hooded shadow swept through the grounds of Shiverton Hall, past the maze and the woods, past the boarding houses and the swimming pool covered with a slimy tarpaulin for the winter. Ronnie followed as close as he dared, with Andrew holding his breath behind him.

It came to a stop outside a square, red-bricked building, rather cosier than the other houses they had passed. Just visible among the ivy clinging to the garden wall, a brass plaque read GARNONS. Ronnie and Andrew ducked behind a bush and watched as the figure approached the building, the door swinging open at its command.

'How did it do that?' Ronnie whispered, impressed. 'It didn't even touch the door!'

'That's enough,' Andrew said desperately. 'Come on.'

'No way!'

Ronnie sneaked into the garden, and peeked in through the window.

Andrew, too frightened to remain on his own, joined him.

They were looking in at a hall. A glass trophy cabinet ran along one wall and a grid of old, wooden pigeonholes was fixed on the other. The figure withdrew a parcel from its sleeve, and slotted it into one of the pigeonholes.

'What is that?' Andrew whispered.

'Shhhh! It's coming back!' Ronnie hissed.

Ronnie and Andrew flattened themselves against the building as the hunched silhouette reappeared on the path.

Andrew squeezed his eyes shut, praying they wouldn't be seen. He didn't dare open his eyes until he heard Ronnie's sigh of relief.

The figure retreated into the swirling mist.

'Phew!' he said. 'That was close.'

'Right,' Ronnie said, walking towards the house. 'Let's see what that was all about, then.'

'You can't!' Andrew said, as Ronnie pushed the door open.

'I'm going to put it back,' Ronnie said. 'It's not like I'm stealing it or anything.'

Ronnie strode over to the pigeonhole and brought down the parcel, carefully untying the string which held the brown paper wrapper in place. He looked at its contents dubiously. 'It's just a book!' he said, his disappointment audible.

'See?' Andrew said. 'It's nothing. Now, can we please LEAVE!'

A light suddenly switched on at the top of the stairs and the boys froze. There were footsteps on the landing above them and a man's voice called out, 'Is someone there?'

Ronnie panicked, hurled the book at Andrew and bolted. Andrew, unsure which hole to return the book to, shoved it into his pocket and ran after Ronnie as the footsteps started to descend the staircase.

They sprinted all the way back to their bikes, and pedalled home faster than they ever had in their lives. When they finally arrived back at Andrew's house, Andrew threw his bike down and turned on Ronnie furiously.

'You can be a real idiot, you know that?' he panted.

'Hang on!' Ronnie laughed. 'We're all right, aren't we? No harm done!'

Andrew brought the book out of his pocket and brandished it at Ronnie, who stopped laughing.

'Why didn't you put it back?' Ronnie asked.

'Because you threw it at me and I didn't know where you'd taken it from and there was someone coming!' Andrew yelled.

'All right, chill out,' Ronnie replied. 'We can take it back tomorrow.'

'There's no way I am going back there tomorrow,' Andrew said. 'You have it.'

Ronnie put his hands up innocently. 'Hey,' he said, 'you're the one who took it.'

Andrew looked at his friend disbelievingly.

'It's just an old book,' Ronnie continued. 'I'm sure no one will miss it.'

'Whatever,' Andrew said. He could barely get his door keys out of his jeans, he was so angry.

'Ah, don't be like that!' Ronnie said.

Andrew slotted his key in the door.

'So, see you tomorrow, then?' Ronnie asked, flicking his bicycle bell so that it rang out across the street.

Andrew let himself into the house without replying. Ronnie deserved to stew for at least an evening.

*

Andrew traced his fingers over the scarred cover, then opened the book. He reread the scrawled warning. He knew he shouldn't look, but he felt a powerful, physical desire to do so – like itching a mosquito bite, or picking at a scab – and before he knew it, he turned the page and began to read.

The writing inside looked as old as the cover; it was handwritten in flowing calligraphic lettering, and none of it made much sense to Andrew. He flicked through the pages until he found a highly decorative page, illustrated in elaborate gold and vermilion ink, with one long word at the centre that he did not recognise. He read the word over a few times, trying to make sense of it.

The room grew colder still, until suddenly Andrew was aware that his breath was clouding in the air in front of him.

And then the noise came. A faint scratching, like a sharp fingernail on glass.

Andrew dropped the book.

CHAPTER ONE

Pink football boots. If there was ever a present that a fourteen-year-old boy really doesn't want for Christmas, it is a pair of baby-pink football boots with sparkly laces. Arthur stared at them, aghast.

'But they're a limited edition!' May Bannister, his mother, insisted. 'The man in the shop said that all the cool kids are wearing them.'

'The cool kids?' Arthur repeated. 'Wearing these?'

'Yes!' May said impatiently. 'That singer wore them on the telly. You know the one – the guy with the leather shorts.'

Rob and Arthur stared at their mother blankly.

May pressed on quickly. 'And the boy in the shop, the one with the trendy haircut, said they're limited edition. All the boys are after a pair.'

'I think he may have been having you on,' Arthur said, turning them over. 'They've got fairies on them.'

'And don't forget the glittery laces,' Rob, Arthur's eleven-year-old half-brother, said gleefully. 'Nothing more manly than pink glittery laces.'

Arthur couldn't help but giggle, and then Rob joined in, and May threw up her hands in despair.

'Why didn't I have girls?' she groaned. 'I've no idea what I did to deserve two horrible boys. I'd have known what to get for girls.'

'It's all right, Mum,' Arthur said. 'At least I won't get them mixed up with anyone else's back at house.'

'*Back at house*,' Rob parroted. Rob found Arthur's boarding-school lingo ridiculous. 'Why don't you just say, "Back at *my* house" or "Back at *the* house"?'

Arthur shrugged. 'That's just what everyone calls it.'

'It's stupid,' Rob said.

'Well, I like it,' their mother said, sensing trouble brewing. 'I think it's lovely and old-fashioned.'

Arthur and Rob had always bickered, but since Arthur had received the scholarship to the illustrious Shiverton Hall the term before, she had grown much more sensitive to it. After all, Arthur was hardly ever at home, and she wanted the boys to get along when they were together.

'You should be glad your brother's so happy at his new school,' May whispered loudly to Rob. 'Especially after what happened at the last one.'

12

'Mum!' Arthur said, going purple.

'What?' Rob said innocently. 'You mean the fact he nearly killed the school bullies with a brick?'

'Robbie!' May gasped. 'He did not nearly kill –'

'He did!' Rob replied.

'Look,' May said, 'those boys are perfectly all right –'

'Apart from a couple of scars –'

'Yes, well, what are a few scars? They tried to drown Arthur!'

Arthur stood up abruptly. 'Can we stop now?' he asked.

'Of course we can,' said May. 'Sorry, petal. Rob, apologise to your brother!'

'Sorry, Arthur,' Rob said, completely insincerely.

May changed the subject. 'I've still got the receipt, Arthur. You can exchange the football boots if you like.'

'No, Mum,' Arthur said. 'Actually, I think they're kind of cool.' He stuck his tongue out at his brother and slipped them on.

After a huge Christmas dinner, the family crashed out in front of the telly, until Rob's Brussels sprout farts became too much to bear and they all ran screaming and clutching their noses to their bedrooms to escape the smell.

Arthur had a lot of reading to do before going back to Shiverton Hall; he was determined to get on the right side of the dreaded Professor Long-Pitt this term. Long-Pitt was his English teacher and the headmistress of the

13

school. Pretty terrifying at the best of times, Long-Pitt had taken an instant dislike to Arthur and had set out to make his life a misery from the moment he arrived. Although Arthur would have liked nothing more than to dunk her into Shiverton Hall's freezing, green fountain, he had made a promise to himself that he would be a model student and make sure she had no reason whatsoever to stick him in detention. She was, after all, a distant relative of his, a fact revealed to him by his housemaster, Doctor Toynbee, at the end of last term.

It turned out that Arthur's mysterious scholarship to Shiverton Hall was even stranger than he had first thought. His late father, a man he had never met and whose surname his mother had previously refused to tell him, had, according to Doctor Toynbee, been an Australian named David Shiverton and a direct (albeit illegitimate) descendant of Lord Frederick Shiverton himself, the murderous aristocrat who built the hall in the eighteenth century. David Shiverton had died young, as so many of the male Shiverton descendants had, leaving only one child, Arthur, a boy who didn't even know his father's name. When Toynbee had discovered this, he had felt it only fair to invite Arthur to the school; Toynbee had read about the terrible business at Arthur's previous school in the papers and felt that Arthur deserved a second chance. Long-Pitt had taken some persuading, but had relented, and they had offered him the scholarship, deciding it was best not to tell Arthur about his unusual connection to the school.

All of that changed, however, when Arthur and his friends were targeted by a strange and powerful phantom, and Toynbee felt it wise to come clean.

Only Toynbee and Long-Pitt knew of Arthur's true heritage; Arthur hadn't even told his friends. Given the reputation of the family, and the curse that was said to be on the Shiverton bloodline, he thought it might be sensible to keep it to himself. The students had already discovered the violent incident at his previous school; if they knew who his father was it would be enough to make him a loner for life. Arthur had not asked his mother about David Shiverton, although he had wanted to many times during the holidays. It would be too difficult to explain how he had come by the information, without revealing the phantom, and he was certain that his mother would never let her son put another foot inside Shiverton Hall if she suspected that he was in danger.

Sometimes he wondered why he wanted to go back there himself. It was no coincidence that the strange supernatural element of the school, dormant for so many years, had reawakened on his arrival there. But then he thought about George, his lanky, ghost-obsessed best friend, and Penny and Jake, and even Xanthe, whose bonkers hairstyles and love of homework hid a surprising

15

brave streak. They were the reason Arthur was going back, and he couldn't wait to see them.

George had been texting Arthur constantly with updates about his Christmas holiday in Scotland. He had fallen down a mountain after accidentally drinking some sherry and sustained a black eye of such oozing disgustingness that his grandfather refused to look at him unless he was wearing an eyepatch.

Penny had called Arthur earlier that day in desperation and had threatened to run away from home. Her enormous family lived in a freezing, dilapidated castle and her mother had entirely forgotten that it was Christmas. Once someone reminded her she had wrapped up some dusty old knick-knacks and tried to pass them off as presents. Penny had received a brass doorknob, but her poor younger brother Sage had really got a bum deal: a pair of his father's moth-eaten old pants. Christmas lunch had been baked beans on toast, accompanied by a highly unusual rendition of 'Jingle Bells' from one of her seven siblings. Apparently, Penny had spent a fair bit of the meal with bread stuffed in her ears to block out the din.

Arthur had been no help at all, giggling helplessly as Penny described her father's attempt to play Father Christmas wearing one of his wife's red dresses and a striped sock as a hat.

'Don't you dare laugh!' Penny had threatened, as

Arthur started snorting. 'I'm going to call Jake and talk to someone sensible instead.'

Poor Jake. Arthur had been wondering how his Christmas had been. Jake's mother had been struggling with mental illness ever since Jake was little, and Jake had looked after her ever since his father had left them. Jake lived in London too, and Arthur had offered to come over and help, but Jake was extremely proud, and his mother did not like visitors.

Xanthe had written Arthur a letter in a purple glitter pen and covered it in stickers. It went into great detail about the science camp she had been attending and the many prizes she had won while she was there. She had also sent a photograph of herself that she'd cut out of a newspaper. It showed her leaning forward in a wheelchair, her legs still in plaster after she'd fallen out of a window the previous term, and clutching one of the trophies she'd won. There was another person in the photo, a slight, bespectacled boy holding a smaller trophy, who Xanthe was shamelessly elbowing out of the picture. She had suggested in her letter, with only the smallest hint of desperation, that Arthur frame the photograph and put it beside his bed. He had settled for his pin-board instead and it made him laugh every time he saw it. He glanced up at the photo now as he prepared for bed. Xanthe could be pretty batty at times – she was wearing lurid pink dungarees and her hairstyle would have looked bizarre on a porcupine, let alone a human being – but she was also one of the cleverest and most loyal people he knew.

Arthur changed into his pyjamas, and once again tried to get cracking on Long-Pitt's endless reading list. It wasn't going very well. He had already begun to snooze on page one of *The Picture of Dorian Gray* when he was startled by the sound of something striking his bedroom window. He sat up in his bed and listened.

There it was again.

Arthur got out of bed and crept to the window, his heart racing. Their flat was on the third floor of a high-rise, and they reached their front door via a concrete walkway, but that was on the floor below and nowhere near within reach of his window.

Arthur waited, holding his breath. His mother would be asleep by now, and Rob would be far too full to be bothered to play a trick on his brother at this time of night. Something struck the windowpane again. Arthur tore open the curtains, and yelped when he saw a face staring back at him.

He laughed nervously when he realised that it was his own face, reflected in the glass. He pulled himself together and peered into the darkness. But he could only see the wet street below, orange in the lamplight and deserted.

Then came the knock at the front door. Arthur felt his skin tighten. His first instinct was to call his mother, but then he shook himself. He was fourteen and the man of the house since Rob's dad, Arthur's stepfather, had gone off to open a pub in Leeds with his new girlfriend. Arthur drew himself to his full height and went downstairs with as much swagger as he could muster. He threw open the front door before he had time to change his mind, and poked his head out into the walkway.

Nothing.

'You!'

Arthur jumped and whirled around. Standing next to him was an old man with a battered stick and a frayed argyle jumper. Arthur sighed with relief.

'Mr Croomb,' he said. 'What are you doing out here?'

Mr Croomb looked at Arthur accusingly. 'What are *you* doing out here?'

Arthur smiled politely; Mr Croomb had been their neighbour for many years, and he still mistrusted the boys, behaving as though they might knock him over and try to steal his pension at any moment.

'Well, boy?' Croomb demanded. 'Up to no good? I saw you eyeing my silver clock from the window last week. Don't think I didn't notice. You've always wanted my silver clock.'

'Someone knocked on our door,' Arthur explained patiently, ignoring the accusation. 'I came to see who it was. Was it you, Mr Croomb?'

'Me? Knock on your door? Why would I do that?'

'I don't know,' Arthur sighed.

'Are you trying to trick me, boy?' Croomb said, jabbing his stick at Arthur. 'Get me out here and then bash me over the head and take my clock, is that it? I'll bash *you* over the head!'

'Oi!' Arthur yelled, hopping out of Croomb's range. 'What are you doing?'

Croomb raised his stick over his head, the silver handle glinting in the light from the neighbours' flashing Christmas display. Arthur covered his head with his hands to cushion the blow. But none came. When Arthur looked back up, Mr Croomb was frozen, his stick poised in mid-air, whimpering and staring at a fixed point behind Arthur. Arthur turned, but could not see what Mr Croomb was looking at.

'S-sorry, boy,' Mr Croomb stammered. 'Happy Christmas.'

Arthur had no idea what was going on. 'Er . . . Happy Christmas, Mr Croomb,' he replied.

Croomb nodded, and scuttled back into his flat, slamming his front door behind him.

Arthur shook his head. 'Absolutely nuts,' he said to himself as he turned back towards his front door. But there was already someone in it.

A huge, broad figure in an oily, black raincoat stood between Arthur and his flat. His face was obscured by a leather hood, which reminded Arthur of the chilling illustrations he had seen of medieval hangmen in Toynbee's

20

history class. Arthur could see the bloodshot eyes glittering behind the hood's slits.

Arthur crept backwards towards Mr Croomb's window; the hooded man remained motionless. Mr Croomb was watching from behind his yellowing curtains, and ducked out of sight when Arthur looked at him imploringly. 'Mr Croomb,' Arthur whispered, banging on the window with one fist, still facing the man. 'Mr Croomb, open the door.'

Mr Croomb pulled his curtains tightly shut and turned off the lights.

The man laughed.

'What do you want?' Arthur asked, as calmly as he could.

The man took two enormous strides towards Arthur and in a moment, had him crushed against the wall with one hairy arm. He reached up with his other hand, and Arthur flinched, expecting a blow to his face. But instead, the man ripped off his hood.

If the hood was frightening, it was nothing compared to what it concealed. The man's face was horribly scarred. Burned, hacked apart, tendons and teeth and an eye socket all exposed and bonded thickly together with pink warped scar tissue, like meat suspended in jelly.

'Why don't you scream?' the man said.

Arthur could see that his tongue was partially missing, and it gave him a blunt, strange, grunting way of speaking, drool seeping from the corners of his twisted mouth. Arthur could barely understand him.

'I said, "Why don't you scream?"' he repeated, crushing Arthur harder against the wall.

'My family,' Arthur choked. 'I don't want them to hear. I don't want them to come down.'

The man's lips moved into an approximation of a smile, and he released Arthur.

'Then I trust I can count on you to stay quiet and not run away?' he growled.

Arthur nodded.

The man looked at Arthur and chuckled. 'Think you're brave, then?' he spat. 'After a few moments at that place, think you're brave?'

Arthur frowned. 'What?'

The man stepped menacingly close to Arthur. 'Shiverton Hall,' he grunted.

'I don't understand,' Arthur said.

The man laughed.

'What do you want? Why are you here?' Arthur asked.

The man glared at Arthur.

'Think of me as a friendly warning,' he answered finally.

'A warning about what?'

The man scratched at his raw face and Arthur winced. The man caught Arthur's reaction and lowered his hand self-consciously.

'Make an excuse to your mother, call the school and tell them you aren't going back.'

'Why?'

'No use asking "why". Just do it,' he growled.

'No,' Arthur replied steadily.

'No?' The man slammed Arthur against the wall again, twice as hard this time, his arm pinning Arthur's neck against the bricks. For a moment Arthur thought the man was going to throttle him, but then he was released suddenly, and he tumbled to the ground clutching his bruised throat. The man looked down at him with a sneer.

'Who sent you here?' Arthur asked.

'What do you mean?' the man replied. 'No one sent me.'

'Why did you come, then?'

The man stepped on Arthur's hand with a heavy boot. The pain was so intense Arthur thought he would have to scream.

'No more questions,' the man said. 'I have come to tell you what you need to know. Be grateful that I have.'

'Grateful?' Arthur nearly laughed.

'Yes. Grateful.' The man looked steadily at Arthur.

He opened his twisted mouth to elaborate when the sound of sirens filled the cold air. Arthur glanced over at Mr Croomb's window; Mr Croomb stared back at him, the phone in his hand.

The man cursed and pulled on his hood roughly. 'You tell anyone I was here, you'll regret it,' the man growled.

Arthur nodded.

'Now, take my advice,' he snarled at Arthur. 'Take it or be damned.'

With one sudden movement, he hoisted his bulk over the balcony wall and disappeared. Arthur rushed over to peer at the paving stones beneath, but there was no sign of him. Not even a footprint in the rain.

The police woke his family, and they piled down sleepily. Arthur maintained that Mr Croomb had been imagining things, and luckily for him, it was not the first time his neighbour had bothered the police with strange complaints. The police went away, leaving Mr Croomb staring accusingly at Arthur as he retreated into his flat.

Arthur didn't have the energy to feel guilty.

CHAPTER TWO

'What. Is. THAT?' Penny cried gleefully.

George threw himself down on the Garnons library sofa nonchalantly.

'An eyepatch,' he replied, coolly examining his finger-nails.

'AN EYEPATCH!' Penny squealed. 'Is it a fashion statement?'

'No.'

'Have you become a pirate?'

'No.'

'Then what happened?'

'I *may* have drunk some of my Great-Aunt Tessa's sherry and *accidentally* fallen down a mountain,' George said quietly.

Penny stood stunned for a moment.

'Oh dear, I have to sit down,' she replied as she collapsed, giggling, into a chintz armchair, her mass of blonde curls bouncing behind her.

'It's very alluring, Penny,' George replied angrily. 'It makes me look like a dashing, devil-may-care master of the ocean.'

'No.' Penny shook her head.

'But –' George said.

'Nope. Off.' Penny stuck out her hand and George handed her the eyepatch.

'Your eye is completely fine!' Arthur said.

'Yeah . . . well, it . . . it wasn't fine a week ago,' George stammered.

'A week! You've been wearing this scabby thing for a week and there's been nothing wrong with your eye!' Penny gasped.

'It makes me look cool, OK?' George snapped. 'And what about you? Who'd choose to wear a dress covered in bugs and plants?'

Penny looked down at her printed dress.

'Oh, who am I kidding?' George sighed. 'You look amazing.'

Penny giggled again.

'Can I have my eyepatch back now?' George asked, grasping for it.

'NO!' Arthur and Penny shouted in unison.

'Where is Jake?' Arthur asked, as they settled down

26

with their cups of tea and last term's mouldy biscuits.

'I haven't really heard much from him these hols,' George replied.

'I hope things are all right at home,' Penny said. 'After everything that happened last term he could have done with a rest.'

'Ha!' A hoarse voice from the door replied. 'I was in a coma for weeks, the last thing I needed was a rest.'

'Jake!' Penny cried, springing up and enveloping him in an enormous hug. He hugged her back awkwardly and smiled at the others.

Jake was unusual-looking at the best of times, with his white-blond hair and pale skin, but now he looked older, and had the haunted, blueish tinge of someone who hadn't slept in a while.

'Are you OK, Jake?' Arthur asked. 'You look a bit . . . knackered.'

Jake smiled tightly. 'I'm fine,' he replied. 'Just need a cup of tea.'

Penny passed her mug over to him. 'I like your new glasses,' she said brightly. He was wearing a pair of very thick tortoiseshell frames that slightly overwhelmed his face.

'My last ones got . . . broken,' he said.

'Right.'

They all sat in silence for a while.

'How's your mum?' George asked.

'Not great,' Jake sighed. 'It's good to be back at school – let's put it that way. I think I might just have had one of the worst Christmases in the whole history of Christmas.'

'Perhaps,' Penny said. 'But you, sir, have not seen my father performing an unabridged, one-man production of Charles Dickens's A *Christmas Carol* entirely in the nude.'

Jake sat silently for a moment, his eyes wide, and then burst out laughing. Soon they were all on the floor in a helpless fit of mirth. 'It's not funny!' Penny choked, tears streaming down her face. 'I'll be in therapy for years!'

'What on earth is going on here?'

They sprang to their feet, trying to stop giggling as Doctor Toynbee, the jovial, ancient housemaster of Garnons, and the man who had saved Arthur's life the previous term, poked his head around the door.

'Don't stop on my account!' he chuckled. 'I take it from the rolling around on the carpet that you all had an enjoyable Christmas break?'

'Very much so, thank you, sir,' George replied, his voice wobblingly close to cracking.

'Good-o. Assembly is in fifteen minutes. You might want to calm yourselves down before you walk over to the hall. You know how Professor Long-Pitt feels about jokes.'

*

28

Arthur and his friends hurried through Shiverton Hall's imposing grounds. Past the creaking woods and the patchy, dry maze and the fountain with its hideous mermaid. The hall itself glowered down at them, its gargoyles watching as they scurried by.

'It looks even more welcoming than usual,' Arthur noted, as a particularly repulsive stained glass window depicting a baby roasting on a spit caught the evening light.

The assembly hall was a squat, semi-circular building that was only ever used for school assemblies and the odd half-hearted production of *Annie*. It was already full, and the chatter of a thousand students echoed around the wood-panelled walls. A few heads turned to look at Arthur; no doubt last term's rumours had not yet been forgotten.

'Let them look,' Penny whispered, reading his mind. 'They'll get bored of it after a while.'

Just as they were taking their seats, a shrill, lisping voice squealed, 'Arthur!' from across the room. A few people giggled as Xanthe hopped gracelessly through the crowd towards them. She had only just had her casts off, having broken both of her legs the previous term, and she was still rather wobbly. 'Make room for me, will you?' she hissed at the poor first year who had the temerity to be sitting next to Arthur, and then turned to Arthur with a lovelorn smile, her braces sparkling in the fluorescent light from above.

'Hello, Arthur,' she breathed. 'Do you mind if I sit here?'

'Doesn't look like he has a choice,' George muttered.

Xanthe glared at him and parked herself in the vacated seat, snuggling close to Arthur as the lights dimmed.

Long-Pitt took the stage like a spider unfurling itself from a crack.

The room hushed immediately as she began her welcome speech. Arthur remembered her speech from last term, which had been interrupted by a deranged ex-pupil who had tried desperately to warn them about their imaginary friends. They should have listened to him, for the 'imaginary friends' had turned out to be a dangerous Amicus phantom that had nearly been the death of quite a few students, including Arthur. He wondered whether today's speech would be as eventful.

Long-Pitt was not a compelling public speaker, preferring to list her way through the term's many events and timetables as joylessly as possible while the students around her slowly lost the will to live. This term's speech mostly focused on the coming weeks' 'Wednesday Afternoon Activities' (or 'WAAs', as Penny called them, because they were so boring they made you cry like a baby). There were many options for the students, including writing for the school paper, rather grandly entitled *The Whisper*, which mostly included a collection of terrible cartoons drawn by George and some exposés of the quality of school food in the dining hall. Pupils could also choose to paint sets for the school play, pay visits to the local community, work in the Grimstone bakery, clear rubbish from the hedgerows, go kayaking in the freezing lake or help out at Grimstone Primary School.

'This year,' Long-Pitt said with a thin smile, 'I shall be allocating the options at random.'

The students groaned.

'Last year so many of you wanted to work at the bakery that Mrs Thomas was quite overwhelmed. Inexplicably, it appears that testing her cakes was more appealing than removing litter from the side of the road, so I have decided it is fairer that I make the decision for you. You will find the details of your activity in your pigeonholes back at house.'

'Great,' Arthur muttered. 'It'll be straight in the freezing lake for me.'

'In rather exciting news,' Long-Pitt continued, sounding not in the least excited, 'the school has been bequeathed a most extraordinary painting by Gainsborough, which I'm sure many of you will look forward to seeing. It will be hanging in the school library from tomorrow.'

'A painting!' George whispered. 'Why doesn't anyone bequeath us something useful like a telly?'

'There is one final thing,' Long-Pitt said. For the first time since coming to Shiverton Hall, Arthur noticed

Long-Pitt looking uncertain. 'As some of you who live locally will know, a boy from Grimstone went missing over the holidays.'

The hall filled with whispering.

'I do not wish to alarm you,' Long-Pitt continued, her voice ever so slightly raised. 'I'm sure that he is perfectly all right and will return home soon, but I ask that you are especially careful when you are in Grimstone, and even on school grounds. If you notice anything unusual then please report it to a member of staff immediately.'

Arthur looked over at his friends. Were they thinking the same thing? From the expressions on their faces, it would appear that they were: the Shiverton curse was never far from any of their minds.

'There is another piece of bad news, I'm afraid. The head of the art school has decided not to come back this term.'

This seemed to disturb the hall even more.

'I know that she was well liked, and I'm sure we will all miss her greatly, but it seems we have found ourselves a rather distinguished replacement. Mr Inigo Cornwall, who I'm sure you have all heard of, will be gracing us with his presence this term.'

At this pronouncement a man burst out from the curtains behind Long-Pitt. Handsome and tanned, he wore sunglasses and a pair of purple trousers that by anyone's standards would be considered too tight.

'Who on earth is he?' Arthur whispered to Penny as Cornwall sauntered out on to the stage to great applause.

'Inigo Cornwall?' Penny asked incredulously. 'Famous artist, used to be married to that supermodel, puts heads in jars and things.'

'Oh yeah,' Arthur said, vaguely recalling seeing him in the paper.

Cornwall yawned and gave a nonchalant wave as the students continued to clap and whoop.

Arthur could have sworn that, at the back of the stage, in the shadows, he saw Long-Pitt roll her eyes.

CHAPTER THREE

B ack at Garnons, George and Arthur discussed Cornwall. They were sitting in Arthur's rickety attic room,
sharing a box of salted fudge that George had brought
back from Scotland.

'It looked like Long-Pitt wasn't that thrilled to see him,'
Arthur said.

'No,' George agreed, his mouth full of fudge, 'but then,
she's not really that thrilled about anything.'

'And what about the boy who went missing?' Arthur
asked. 'Do you know what happened?'

'Ah,' George said, getting up to look out of Arthur's
round window. 'That.'

'Why do I get the feeling that you are about to say something mysterious?' Arthur laughed.

'Because, my friend,' George said, casually tossing a bit

of fudge into his mouth, 'I am an intriguing fellow –'

'Your flies are undone,' Arthur cut in.

George glanced down. 'So they are.'

'Anyway, what happened?' Arthur asked.

'His name was Andrew Farnham,' George began. 'He was thirteen, clever, happy at school, lived in Grimstone all his life. He disappeared just before Christmas.'

'That's terrible,' Arthur replied.

'Awful,' George agreed. 'His parents said he had started acting a bit funny about a week before his disappearance. Paranoid, a bit spooked, but he wouldn't say what was wrong. Then, when they woke up on Christmas Eve he was gone.'

Arthur shivered.

'Grandpa was very interested, as you can imagine,' George continued.

'Of course he was,' Arthur sighed.

George's grandfather was another Shiverton ex-pupil, and a friend of Toynbee's. He had written several enormous tomes on the school's more unusual aspects. His book, *Studies into the Supernatural and Preternatural at Shiverton Hall and Its Surrounds*, contained many ghoulish stories about the hall's past, and George was always itching to crack it open and read one to anyone who would listen.

'So, what does your grandfather think happened?' Arthur asked.

'Oh, he has a lot of theories, as you might imagine! Children have been going missing in Grimstone since the place was built. He says it could be another phantom, or a banshee, or a hobgoblin, or even Skinless Tom.'

Arthur shuddered at the name.

'But he has no idea. There's nothing to go on. Not so much as a drop of ectoplasm.'

'Do they think that someone took him? Like, kidnapped him?' Arthur asked.

'To be honest I think kidnapping would be the best he could have hoped for,' George replied quietly. 'Worse things have happened here, after all.'

Arthur was about to reply when his bedroom door was kicked open with a crash. Arthur and George jumped, as the silhouettes of the hideous Forge triplets appeared in the room. Arthur readied himself for a fight, while George suddenly found something fascinating to stare at on Arthur's bookshelf.

The Forge triplets were enormous, and looked as though a child had fashioned three identical figures out of a gigantic tin of corned beef. Pink, angry, snobbish and only distinguishable by their noses, which had all broken in different directions during their many sporting activities, the Forges loathed Arthur.

It came as a surprise, therefore, when Dan Forge, the leader of the trio and the brother who hated Arthur the most, forced a grimace of a grin and said mechanically,

'Hello, Arthur, how was your holiday?'

George and Arthur stared at Dan, waiting for the insult or dead arm that would surely follow. Neither came. Dan continued as his brothers shifted uncomfortably behind him. 'Looking forward to playing football with you.' Sweat was standing out on Dan's brow from the effort of this politeness. 'Why don't we all walk there together tomorrow?'

'What, so you can drag me into the woods and give me a kicking like last time?' Arthur blazed.

'No,' Dan said slowly. 'Because we'd like to be friends. Wouldn't we, guys?'

Dan's brothers grunted in agreement.

'Riiiiight,' Arthur replied, utterly bemused. 'I think I'll pass on that, cheers.'

Dan's right eye twitched. He looked as though he wanted nothing more than to throw Arthur out of the window. Instead, he nodded.

'OK, then. See you around . . .' Dan took a deep breath and shuddered before he added, '*mate.*'

The other two Forge brothers looked as shocked at this term of endearment as Arthur and George did. They trudged off, leaving Arthur gaping.

'Wh-what. On. EARTH?' Arthur stammered.

'Hey, can you blame them?' George replied. 'They know what you did to the last boys who tried to bully you. They probably don't want to end up in hospital.'

'Don't joke about that, George,' Arthur said.

'Sorry,' George said. 'But at least you have one less thing to worry about.'

'Either that or they're planning something.'

'You might be the next person to disappear – I wouldn't put it past them!' George said, starting on the second layer of fudge.

Arthur frowned. 'What do *you* think happened to that boy?'

George shrugged. 'Andrew Farnham? Beats me. This isn't the first time something like this has happened. I mean, the reason the Shiverton curse started in the first place was because all those girls went missing –'

'Because Lord Shiverton murdered them and failed to realise one of their mothers was a witch,' Arthur interrupted. 'I remember, kind of a difficult story to forget.'

'But children have been going missing from Grimstone for centuries. Way before Lord Shiverton built the hall too. Don't forget, there was a reason Lord Shiverton was attracted to this area – it's a dark place.'

'You don't need to tell me,' Arthur replied.

'Don't I?' George said in a mysterious voice, and Arthur knew immediately that George had already memorised one of his grandfather's stories for this precise occasion.

'Go on, then,' Arthur sighed.

GREY MARY

The Trapper family had lived in Grimstone for many generations, eking out a living on the fringes of the town, all of them crammed into a tiny, dirt-floor cottage in the kind of squalid poverty that was common for rural families in Elizabethan times. Mrs Trapper had died giving life to her twelfth child (and the fifth that survived past the cradle) and so it was up to Mr Trapper and his aged mother to care for them all. Mr Trapper was a tall man, with a stoop and a single tooth, which jutted from his mouth accusingly. He sorely resented having so many children underfoot and often said that he would have much preferred it had all of them perished at birth. There was one child that he particularly resented having to care for, a girl called Mary, who was not his own, but some waif his soft-hearted wife had brought home many years before, and who had somehow become a part of the family.

The Trapper children were sent out to work the moment they could put one foot in front of the other. The boys would help at the blacksmith's, coming home with a single clammy coin between them at the end of the week, while Mary and Ruth would scrub the floors at the tavern until their hands bled. Mr Trapper was a poacher, and a bad one at that, and the family mostly had to make do with a single, mangy rabbit every other day. Mr Trapper would eat the best part of the meat, old Ma Trapper would gnaw on the legs, while the children had to make do with the guts and heart and eyes.

One by one, the children became as cold and calloused and hard as their father. But none had become so frozen and hardened as Mary.

Perhaps it was the fact that Mr Trapper never let her forget that she was not a true Trapper, or the fact that old Ma Trapper enjoyed beating Mary the hardest with her gnarled broomstick, but as Mary grew, she became wilier and crueller than the others. She was uncommonly tall for her age, indeed for any age, and had to half-crouch inside their small cottage, her long, dark hair almost brushing the floor. Painfully thin, and with skin of a grey, waxy hue, the sight of Mary walking down the dusty Grimstone path at dusk caused her neighbours to shudder. Even Mr Trapper, who was reputed to have throttled a wild boar with his bare hands in his youth, began to fear being alone with her.

Soon the owner of the tavern asked that Mary stop coming to scrub the floors. She was scaring the customers away, he

40

said. With no way of earning her keep, Mary had given Mr Trapper the excuse he needed to be rid of her for good. He cast her out of the cottage and bolted the door behind her. Left to the bitter winter with only a thin shawl and her long hair to keep her warm, Mary disappeared into the woods.

If the other children felt guilty about Mary's expulsion, they dared not speak of it to their father, and the shame of their betrayal was relieved somewhat by the fact that they had to divide their supper with one person fewer. Soon winter became spring, and as the roots started to struggle their way out of the hard ground, the Trapper family began to forget that Mary had ever been one of their party; they had lost brothers and sisters before, after all.

It was then that the first Grimstone child went missing, while gathering bluebells in the woods to sell at the market. The child was the eight-year-old daughter of the tavern owner and would not have been a stranger to the Trapper children, who helped with the search themselves, shouting her name throughout the village. It would be the first of many searches that spring.

A few days into the search, Mr Trapper went to check one of his rabbit traps, deep in the woods, and discovered something that made him feel quite peculiar. In the pale bark of the ash trees, about seven feet above the ground, were long, deep scratchings.

What could have scored the wood so deep, and so high up? He wondered. There were tales of the Grimstone woods, of course, of the witches that hid there to escape burning, but he had been trapping there since he was a boy and had never seen anything suspicious.

He reached up his hand to feel the marks, and discovered something embedded in the wood. He drew it out, and to his disgust, found that it was a long, yellow talon, about the length of a dagger and just as sharp.

It was no animal claw, that he knew; it was a fingernail.

Mr Trapper took it at once to the tavern, not because he had a care for the missing child, but because the tavern owner had promised a hot supper to any man with evidence of his daughter. Mr Trapper got his hot supper, and the news of the fingernail travelled like quicksilver through the village. People came in their dozens to the tavern just to examine it; in fact, it proved so popular that the landlord's canny wife began to charge for a look.

Was it a monster? the villagers wondered. A witch?

When the second child went missing in the woods a few weeks after the first, Grimstone began to hum with panic. It was a witch, they were certain, a child-eating witch in the woods. Children were forbidden to leave their homes. Their mothers kept them close to their skirts, and their fathers slept by their beds. All except for Mr Trapper, of course, who was more concerned about foolishly giving the lucrative fingernail away in exchange for a half-rotten pie.

In the middle of a warm May night, the village baker was at his furnace, preparing the day's bread. He was often the only man awake in Grimstone at that hour, aside from the odd passing traveller or drunkard lurching home. The baker whistled as he worked the dough and shovelled loaves into the oven. On that night, he was whistling a new tune, one that he had picked up from the tavern a few evenings before, a jaunty song about a pretty girl.

As he was merrily kneading a few currants into some buns, he smelled burning, a dreaded thing for any baker, and, cursing, he rushed over to the ovens. He peered in, but found his loaves perfectly golden, with not a scorched top among them.

But the smell of burning was still there, catching the back of his throat. It wasn't burning bread, he realised, but an altogether more unpleasant odour: that of burning hair. He shuddered. He remembered the smell from his boyhood, when his mother had taken him to watch one of Queen Mary's heretic burnings. The smell of the hair burning was always a good sign, his mother had said, because it meant that the flames of the pyre had finally reached the heretics' heathen heads.

The baker staggered out of his kitchen, only to find that the stench was even more cloying outside. He peered down the dark street. Perhaps an untended bedroom candle had set a woman's hair alight, he thought, but he could see no flames and hear no shrieking from any of the houses. A little nervous now, the baker turned back to his work, quietly whistling, when he heard the same tune, whistled back to him from the darkness at the other end of the street. The baker stopped

43

abruptly and turned. The whistling continued, but he could not see the source of it, and although he was not a superstitious man, he felt very strongly that he must not call out.

A little way down the street, a door opened, and the small figure of a girl crept out and walked slowly towards the music. The baker whispered to her, 'Stop! Stop, child!' but the child did not heed him, and he dared not go after her. Then another door opened, and another, and two more children peered out, and walked barefoot in their bedclothes into the night. The baker stared after them.

Was that a shape he could see?

The figure was as tall as a tree and thin as a reed, with long hair that floated around it like tentacles. Its outstretched arms clasped the children to its side, one by one.

Before the baker could cry out, the whistling stopped, and the burning smell disappeared with it.

The figure and the children were nowhere to be seen.

The baker's story of the strange figure held the village in a grip of terror. Five children were missing, and the villagers began to cast around desperately for an explanation. It was the landlord's wife who first brought up Mary Trapper, and her uncommon height, and her strange, grey skin. It was not long until the whole of Grimstone took up her name.

Grey Mary. That is what they called her. Grey Mary was coming to steal their children.

Soon children were seeing Grey Mary everywhere, grasping out at them in their sleep from beneath their beds, roaming the streets at night, whistling a flat, hollow tune. Every child in the village lived in terror that she would snatch them away in the night.

All except two.

Farrus and Peter were twins, and the sort of boys that other children avoided. Small, pale and sickly, and always whispering to each other in a strange, shared language, they drifted around the village, plucking wings from butterflies and twisting the heads off ants. Even their mother was unsettled by them, and prayed fervently every night that they would change.

The twins didn't care that children were disappearing; in fact, they were rather enjoying the hysteria and the spectacle that Grey Mary had brought to their dull little village. As far as they were concerned, their neighbours had it coming to them. Their mother hushed them fearfully when they said such things, but they ignored her. They wanted to see the witch for themselves, and no amount of whining from Mother was going to stop them.

In the middle of a crisp, moonless night, they crept from their cottage as their parents slept, making their way to the woods.

The following morning, their mother found them in their beds, covered in blood. She stifled a scream and ran to them. Peter's blue eyes opened, bright and beady against the red that caked his face.

'Get off me,' he hissed, and his mother staggered back in surprise.

Farrus giggled.

'Boys,' she whispered, 'what have you been doing?'

'We've been in the woods,' Farrus replied, with a strange, sly smile.

'Are you injured?' she asked.

They frowned.

'The blood,' she said.

Farrus and Peter said something to each other in their private language and laughed.

'What are you saying?' Their mother was annoyed.

'Blood?' Farrus giggled. 'This isn't blood, Mother. It's mud.'

Their mother had not been into the woods since she was a girl, but she remembered that the clay in the soil did give the ground a red, bloody hue.

She dared not tell their father, who was rather free with his fists, and so she made them wash with a cloth, and begged them not to return to the woods.

The twins did not listen. Every few nights they would disappear from their room, and when they returned in the morning they would be covered in the red mud, and another child would be missing. Not knowing what else to do, their mother would wake on their return and creep past her sleeping husband to the twins' room, to find her sons smiling their curious smiles, and would force them to wash.

She began to notice changes: they were growing taller, stronger, their thin hair turning thick and lustrous, and their eyes clear. Desperate to do something, she confronted her sons in the middle of the night and begged them to see sense, to stop going to the woods, to listen to their poor mother. Peter turned to her and laughed. 'We have a new mother now,' he sneered. She dared not ask him what he meant.

As dawn broke the following morning, their mother crept out of the house to speak to the parson. She was convinced her children had been possessed by the witch and were somehow doing her bidding. Her sons had been sleeping when she left the house, but as she hastened up the path to the parsonage she saw something that almost made her faint with horror. Walking towards the woods, their steps in unison, were the twins. Between them, holding their hands, was a little girl, no more than a toddler.

The mother called out to her sons, but they carried on, laughing and teasing the little girl.

'Stop!' their mother cried.

She ran after them, chasing through the woods, screaming for help, but her sons, and the child between, had disappeared.

The twins and little Betty Archer were the last children to go missing that year. None of the villagers found so much as a hair to help them in their search.

There was no clue as to why, or how, the children had been taken, and the twins' mother remained silent about her sons' possible involvement. What good could it do to speak of it now?

A few weeks later, after a church service for the missing children, the parson overheard one of the Trapper children whispering something to her brother.

'It looks like Mary got what she was after,' the Trapper girl said.

'And what was that?' the parson asked, not minding that he had been caught eavesdropping.

The Trapper girl looked up at him and said, with a toothless grin, 'A family.'

'Creepy,' Arthur said. 'How many children went missing?'

'Thirteen of them altogether,' George replied.

'Thirteen!'

'A witch's dozen,' George said, 'including Farrus and Peter.'

'How on earth does your grandfather find out this stuff?' Arthur asked.

'The parson's diary,' George shrugged. 'The twins' mother confessed everything to him before she died.'

'Thirteen kids abducted by a witch? Sounds a bit far-fetched even for your grandfather,' Arthur chuckled.

'That's what you said last term,' George sighed. 'And look how that turned out.'

CHAPTER FOUR

Shiverton Hall's impressive art block had been built in 1930 by Professor Long-Pitt's grandfather. Made almost entirely of glass and wrought iron, and covered with twisted ivy, it resembled a greenhouse or an enormous birdcage more than it did a school building. It was quite unlike the rest of the school, being a light and friendly sort of place, and after so many lessons in the darkness of Long-Pitt's wood-panelled study and the archaeological clutter of Toynbee's room, Arthur always looked forward to going there in spite of the fact that he had no artistic talent whatsoever.

The vast main classroom was set in an atrium in the middle of the building, and sunlight flooded in through the windows, illuminating past students' work that hung on the walls. There were no desks in the art block, only large paint-spattered tables, and Arthur, Penny, Jake and George settled around one of them, speculating about the famous Mr Cornwall's first lesson. Just as the bells sounded, Xanthe stumbled in, carrying a satchel bursting with books, and slumped down on the stool next to Arthur. 'Have I missed anything?' she whispered. 'I was helping Long-Pitt put away the chairs at break time.'

'No one likes a suck-up, Xanthe,' George sang.

'Everyone loves a suck-up, George,' Xanthe snapped. 'That's why I'm going to be prime minister, and you are going to have to marry a rich, old crone because no one will ever give you a job.'

'How old is this crone exactly?' George asked.

'More importantly, how rich?' Penny giggled.

Just as Xanthe was about to throw her glittery pen at Penny, the doors to the art room opened with a slam, and Cornwall, wearing a pair of enormous sunglasses and some silver trousers that were even tighter than the last pair, staggered into the room rubbing his temples.

He looked up slowly, and jumped when he saw a sea of expectant faces staring back at him.

'What are you all doing here?' he groaned.

Someone cleared their throat. There was a pause.

'Um . . .' Xanthe said, 'we're your second-year class – you're supposed to be teaching us.'

'Teaching you?' Cornwall replied, bewildered. 'What am I supposed to be teaching you?'

'Art,' Xanthe replied slowly.

'Oh . . . right . . . yeah,' Cornwall said, smoothing down the worst excesses of his hair. 'OK, everyone, grab a . . .' He stopped and clutched his head. 'You know . . . a . . . thing . . . you put the canvas on it . . .'

'An easel?' Xanthe deadpanned.

'An easel. Exactly. Ten points to you, tiny child.'

'We don't have points here,' Xanthe muttered as she pulled an easel towards the centre of the room. 'And I'm fourteen.'

'What's going on with him?' Arthur whispered to Jake.

'No idea,' Jake sighed. 'He's a conceptual artist – you know, puts heaps of rubbish on the floor, that sort of thing. He's probably never held a paintbrush in his life.'

'This is going to be amazing,' Arthur giggled.

Soon all of the class were standing by their easels in a circle around Cornwall, who, having been fetched a glass of water, was looking a little more sensible.

He took off his sunglasses and winced at the blinding light.

'Right,' he began, 'I'm sure your last art teacher wanted to teach you how to draw an apple, paint a still life, that sort of thing?'

The class nodded.

'Good. Well, I am not going to teach you those things. You don't need to paint to be an artist, OK?'

'What about Michelangelo, sir?' George asked.

Cornwall ignored him.

51

'To be a good artist,' Cornwall continued, 'you need to *feel*.'

Xanthe snorted.

'Out!' Cornwall roared, with surprising ferocity.

'What?' Xanthe replied uncertainly.

'Get out,' he repeated, pointing towards the door. 'I don't mind rebellion, but I can't stand squares. Come back next lesson with an open mind.'

Xanthe, her mouth furiously agape, snatched up her satchel and stormed out.

'Anyone else?' Cornwall challenged.

The class shook their heads.

They spent the rest of the lesson on a series of experimental exercises, drawing with their eyes shut, drawing upside down, drawing with the charcoal in their mouths. When the bell went it seemed as though the class had gone by in a moment.

'No homework,' Cornwall said as the students gathered up their things. 'I don't believe in homework.'

As Arthur and his friends left the art block, George was completely awestruck. 'He's so cool,' he gabbled. 'Did you see his earring? It was a skull with a snake in it!'

'That would have looked great with your pirate eyepatch,' Arthur conceded.

'I know you're taking the mick,' George replied, 'but that earring would actually have looked incredible with my eyepatch.'

'I thought it was a bit ridiculous, all of that "Paint with your gut, not with your eyes" rubbish,' Arthur said.

'I liked it,' Jake said. 'I never got art before, but it feels good to be able to just do what you want. Not have to worry about getting it wrong.'

'Speaking of getting it wrong . . . Xanthe is going to be seething,' Penny giggled. 'A bag of cinder toffee says she's already dobbed Cornwall in to Long-Pitt.'

George and Arthur returned to Garnons at the end of the day to find a thick envelope in each of their pigeonholes. George pulled his out and noted the spidery writing. 'Long-Pitt,' he groaned. 'The Wednesday Afternoon Activities have obviously been allocated.'

Arthur braced himself. 'Picking up dog poo for me, then.'

They tore open the envelopes.

'Oh,' George said, surprised. 'I'm helping supervise the Grimstone Primary football team. I'm terrible at football!'

Arthur looked at his card curiously. 'It says: *Generational Assistance*. And there's a name: *Mrs Todd*. What's this?'

George smiled. 'Ah. Oldie wrangling.'

'That makes even less sense,' Arthur replied.

'You help out an oldie from the village. As in, you're given a Grimstone granny and you go and have tea with them and listen to their stories and get their shopping and things.'

53

'Why don't we swap?' Arthur said. 'I'm good at football and you'd love oldie wrangling. You love tea and stories.'

'Would there be cake?' George asked, tempted.

'They're old people! Of course there'll be cake.'

'OK, done,' George said, swapping his card with Arthur's.

Toynbee appeared from the library, his arms filled with a heap of history books, catching Arthur and George mid-swap.

'Nice try,' Toynbee said, 'but I'm afraid Long-Pitt has forbidden trading. She has allocated every activity personally.'

'Well, she hasn't done a very good job of it,' George replied sulkily.

'Sometimes, Mr Grant, it is a good idea to do things that we are not good at. It is often then that we learn something about ourselves.'

'I'll learn how to get kicked in the shins by a bunch of eight-year-olds,' George grumbled.

Toynbee peered at Arthur's card. 'Oh! Mrs Todd!' he exclaimed. 'Well, Arthur, it seems you've won the lottery. What luck! Do send her my regards. A wonderful woman, wonderful!'

With that, Toynbee wandered off, humming a jolly tune. Arthur and George looked at each other.

'Looks like someone's got a crush!' George said. 'Do you think you get extra credit for matchmaking?'

CHAPTER FIVE

When Wednesday afternoon came, the majority of the students in Arthur's class were grumbling about the activities that they had been allocated. Penny had been signed up to the school newspaper – 'If I have to write a story on late library books I'm going to kill myself' – along with Xanthe, who had already filled a notebook with article ideas. Jake was painting the sets for the school play, supervised by Cornwall, and was looking forward to it more than he'd thought he would be. George was feeling even more glum now that he had discovered he would be coaching football with the Forge triplets.

'You may never see me again,' George said mournfully, as he and Arthur climbed on the rickety old school bus. 'I'll be mounted and put on the wall of the Forges' hunting lodge.'

Arthur shushed George. Dan Forge was making his way towards them at the back of the bus, his brothers filing behind him.

Dan nodded at Arthur and said, through gritted teeth, 'Hello, Arthur. Hope the new term is treating you well?'

Arthur blinked back at Dan; it took him a moment to find his voice. 'Er . . . yes, thanks, Dan.'

'Good-o,' Dan replied, one of his eyes twitching with the effort of being civil. 'Do you mind if we sit with you?' he grunted.

'No,' Arthur said, convinced he was walking straight into a trap.

Dan's gaze transferred to George. 'Get out of my seat, then, cretin,' he sneered.

'I am so excited,' Xanthe lisped, her ponytail bouncing behind her. She had gone for an unusually tame hairstyle that morning in order to look as much like a serious journalist as possible. 'I've always wanted to work for a paper. Breaking stories, fighting corporations, getting the scoop!'

'Steady on, Xanthe,' Penny said. '*The Whisper* is hardly *The Times*, is it? I mean, they publish George's cartoons, for a start. Do you remember the one he did last term about lasagne? It didn't make any sense! He didn't even spell lasagne right.'

'True,' Xanthe admitted darkly. 'But things can change – there's a new editor this term.'

56

The girls opened the door to the newspaper room, and froze on the threshold.

'Oh no,' Xanthe whispered.

Sitting behind the editor's desk was Chukwudi Pike. The son of a billionaire newspaper magnate and a former Miss Nigeria, Chuk Pike was a sixth-former who made every girl in the school go completely soppy at twenty paces. There had been rumours that a girl in the third year had once fainted when he smiled at her in the dining hall. Penny could see why when he looked up at the girls and grinned. 'You must be Penny and Xanthe,' he said. 'Take a seat.'

Penny stammered something incomprehensible and Xanthe, for some unknown reason, curtsied, and then stumbled to a chair.

The Whisper's headquarters consisted of a single, poky room at the top of the main school building. Past issues were pasted all over the walls, going back to the Sixties, with hard-hitting headlines such as: *BREAK TIME SLASHED BY FIVE MINUTES* and *STUDENT WINS THIRD PRIZE IN LOCAL POTTERY COMPETITION.* Penny and Xanthe tried not to stare too obviously at Chuk as they waited for the room to fill up with would-be journalists.

Once the last student had wandered in, Chuk stood up and surveyed his new staff: the selection did not look promising. Apart from Penny and Xanthe, there was a boy named

Hilary, who already had his finger up his nose; a sixth-former called Freya, who was doodling on her hands with a pink felt-tip; a couple of sniggering boys, who were hitting each other with rulers; and a smattering of other disinterested students, who kept on glancing at their watches.

'Right,' Chuk said, 'I know that since Long-Pitt insisted on allocating the WAAs this year, none of you have chosen to be here. I also realise that for the past . . . well, *ever*, *The Whisper* has been a pretty rubbish paper.'

A few of the students nodded in agreement.

'Well, I'd like to change that. As some of you may know, my dad owns a couple of newspapers himself.'

One of the sniggering boys rolled his eyes at this.

'And what he has taught me,' Chuk continued, 'is that there is always a story. I'm not interested in publishing articles about broken vending machines or stale toast rations.'

Chuk walked over to one of the yellowing front pages pinned to the wall and pointed to it. 'September 1973,' he said. 'What does the headline say?'

Xanthe read it out, '*TEA LIMITED TO ONE CUP A DAY.*'

'Right,' Chuk sighed. 'Do you know what else happened that month?'

The students shook their heads.

'A kid went missing from the maze. Just disappeared.' Chuk clicked his fingers. 'Like that. And how about this one?'

Chuk moved to a paper on the other side of the room. '*COSTUMES IN SCHOOL OLIVER PRODUCTION "TOO REVEALING" SAYS VICAR. May 1985.*'

Penny giggled.

'Do you know what else happened in May 1985?' Chuk continued. 'The school bus went missing on a trip to the Lake District. Vanished into thin air. And then turned up again a month later, only none of the kids on it could remember a single thing about where they'd been.'

Chuk now had the entire room rapt – even Hilary had taken his finger out of his nose.

'What I'm saying is,' Chuk said, 'we need to be investigating this stuff. This is what should be going on the front page. A kid went missing in Grimstone over Christmas. What happened to him? The police have no idea. But I want to find out.'

Chuk turned to Penny and Xanthe and smiled. 'How do you girls fancy a trip to Grimstone?'

Arthur looked at the address written on the paper in his hand. 'Mrs Todd, Rose Cottage, Woodland Row, Grimstone.' He had walked up and down Grimstone's quaint, cobbled high street about a hundred times and had absolutely no clue where he was going.

He reluctantly opened the door to Aunt Bessie's Sweet Shop. The little bell tinkled as he entered the fog of cigarillo smoke and sherbet dust that made up the atmosphere of Grimstone's least child-friendly shop. Aunt Bessie stood, as always, behind the counter, sucking on a small, brown cigar, her bleached hair frazzling in all directions. She hadn't bothered to take down the Christmas decorations – in fact, they might even have been from the Christmas before – and they hung limply from the ceiling, gently poking customers in the eye as they entered.

'What do you want?' Aunt Bessie barked.

'I was just wondering, could you direct me to Rose Cottage?' Arthur asked.

'Do I look like a bloody map?' Aunt Bessie sneered, revealing red lipstick all over her yellow teeth.

Arthur sighed. 'Can I have some strawberry laces, then?'

'That's more like it,' said Aunt Bessie as she aggressively shook some strawberry laces on to the scales.

'Do you want bonbons too? We got lots of bonbons.'

'No, I don't really like bonbons, thanks,' Arthur said.

Aunt Bessie glared at him.

'Oh, all right, fine. Some bonbons, then, too,' Arthur huffed.

'Rose Cottage, was it?' Aunt Bessie said, taking a long puff. 'It's up past the high street, just on the lane past the woods. Very hoity-toity, the owner is.'

Arthur rolled his eyes and passed Aunt Bessie a five-pound note.

'I'll keep the change, shall I?' Aunt Bessie asked. 'For my troubles.'

Arthur opened his mouth to protest that it was his pocket money for the whole week, but the look on Aunt Bessie's face made him think better of it.

Arthur made his way up the lane through the woods. He hadn't seen a single house for ten minutes and was now wondering whether Aunt Bessie had been winding him up. He was just about to turn around when he heard rock music being blasted from the path up ahead. Curious, he carried on, following the music as it grew louder and louder.

A little further up the path was a clearing and, within it, a tiny thatched cottage with a bright pink painted door. Around the rambling front garden, tall trees were filled with multi-coloured ribbons and wind chimes, and the lawn itself was covered in garden gnomes. On the little white gate was a plaque bearing the name *Rose Cottage*, and underneath was a handmade sign that read: *Get lost!*

Arthur tentatively walked through the gate and rung the doorbell. There was no response, probably because the Rolling Stones were being played at a deafening volume inside. Arthur followed a gravel path around the cottage, peering in the windows, until he got to the kitchen and spotted an old lady with bright orange hair wearing a green, silk kimono, dancing along to the ancient record player.

She turned, saw Arthur and screamed. Arthur, in his surprise, screamed back. The old lady grabbed a frying pan from the drainer and threw open the window. 'Who the blazes are you?' she demanded, swiping at him with the frying pan.

'Are . . . are you Mrs Todd?' Arthur stammered.

'Who's asking?'

'I'm Arthur,' Arthur said. 'I'm a student at Shiverton Hall. I'll be coming to help you on Wednesday afternoons.'

'Oh Lord,' Mrs Todd groaned. 'They've sent another one, have they? I keep telling them I don't need any help.' She eyed him up and sighed. 'Well, I suppose you'd better come in then, Albert.'

Arthur sat in Mrs Todd's shambolic sitting room, holding a chipped china teacup . He took in the broken piano, and the garish floral curtains, and the dying plants. The walls were filled with absolutely hideous portraits and Mrs Todd noticed Arthur looking at them.

'Ghastly, aren't they?' she said. 'My son does them. No talent whatsoever, poor boy, but one must be encouraging.'

'They're very –' Arthur struggled to find something complimentary – 'arresting.'

'Yes,' Mrs Todd said with half a smile. 'So the school has sent you oldie-wrangling, then? Bad luck. Not much fun for a boy your age to have to spend his afternoons with an old bat like me.'

Arthur didn't know how to respond.

'How is Shiverton, then? Is Long-Pitt still the head-mistress?'

'She is,' Arthur replied.

'Is she still as grim as ever? Why on earth that woman wanted to teach at a school, I'll never know. Hates children!'

'She certainly doesn't like me,' Arthur agreed.

'Oh, she doesn't like anyone. I wouldn't worry about it. Cake?'

Soon Arthur and Mrs Todd were chatting like old friends. Mrs Todd had been an actress, and her mantel-piece was filled with photographs of her as a young woman.

'Absolutely gorgeous, wasn't I?' she said, looking wistfully at a black and white photo of herself dressed as an Egyptian queen. 'Ah, to be young.'

She turned her mascara-caked eyes to Arthur. 'Tell me about yourself, Albert. Tell me about school. Do you have a girlfriend? Boyfriend?'

'Er . . . *girlfriend*,' Arthur stressed. 'No, I don't. The last girl I liked turned out to be . . . well, a bit of a monster.'

'Oh, there are a lot of monsters at Shiverton Hall,' Mrs Todd said with a shudder. 'Haven't been to that place for years – gives me the creeps.'

'It can be pretty creepy,' Arthur admitted.

'You know an acquaintance of mine, an author, went there to write a book once.' She looked down at her lap. 'An awful business,' she said quietly.

'What happened?' Arthur asked.

'I probably shouldn't . . .' Mrs Todd replied. 'It's not a very nice story.'

'I have a friend who would kill me if he knew I'd passed up an opportunity to hear a Shiverton story,' Arthur said.

'Well, all right,' Mrs Todd said, clearly thrilled to have the opportunity to perform. 'Maybe just this once. You're not easily frightened, are you?'

PAYMENT PLEASE

Antony Richmond was a genius. Everyone agreed. His first book, Under Her Feet, was published when he was only nineteen, and he had become an overnight sensation in 1950s London. Under Her Feet was swiftly followed by Ladybird, another hit that took America by storm and made him tremendously rich. But, as with many young men who have seen success too early, Antony Richmond panicked. Every time he sat down to write, he froze. His hand would cramp around his pen and his mind would turn as white and empty as the page in front of him. Soon a year became two, and two became five, and the literary circles in London began to joke about him. A bout of writer's block became 'having an Antony Richmond', and even Richmond's publisher was beginning to lose patience with him.

Richmond decided that he needed to get out of London,

away from his sneering so-called friends and the flashy flat he had bought with his ever-diminishing Ladybird fortune. He chose a place called Deia, a small village on the Spanish island of Majorca. Many beautiful stories had been written about the place and Richmond felt that a bit of warmth in his bones would be just the thing to unblock the ink in his pen.

He took a small, spartan house on a hill, overlooking the glittering sea and the honey-coloured village, and spent his days wandering around the hillside, jotting little notes in a book and drinking wine in the local bar. He had tried to write a few sentences sitting at his desk with the cool breeze blowing the muslin curtains romantically about him, but no matter how glorious the setting, he could not think of a single thing to write.

At his wits' end, and with the summer turning into a drizzly autumn, Richmond started to pack up his things. He would have to get a job teaching at some provincial university, he thought miserably, and eke out the rest of his life as a punchline, occasionally signing tatty paperbacks for old ladies on trains.

As he kicked down the dusty Majorcan street for the last time, there was a rumble in the sky, and soon he was in the thick of a deluge of biblical proportions. He ran for cover and found himself in a cluttered antiques shop that smelled thickly of untreated leather. The shop mostly seemed to be selling broken junk: puppets with their strings cut, chessboards with missing pieces, a doll's house that looked as though a terrible massacre had occurred inside it. Richmond noticed a small, portly woman watching him from the back of the shop.

'Hola,' Richmond said, tipping his hat to her. The lady shrank back further into the shadows. Richmond looked outside; the rain showed no sign of abating. He wondered how long he could politely stay in the shop without being obliged to buy something. The woman glared at him from behind a broken chandelier.

He sighed and looked around for some small knick-knack that he could buy as a token. He had just picked up a hideous, decorative owl when something caught his eye. Just behind the doll's house was a cobwebbed, filthy typewriter. Richmond considered himself something of an aficionado of the machines and had quite a collection of them at home. Even in its obviously poor condition, Richmond could tell that this one was a beauty. He had not seen the make before – Zezia, it read, in curling silver letters above the keyboard. The body of the typewriter seemed to be carved out of some black onyx-like stone and the keys were mother-of-pearl. Richmond blew the cobwebs from it and marvelled for a moment. He felt the collector's thrill, the clammy palms, the racing pulse. He knew that he must have it, and he was determined to get it at a good price. This local woman clearly had no idea what a treasure she was sitting on, and from the way this masterpiece had been left to rot she clearly didn't deserve to know.

Richmond beckoned to her. 'Excuse me,' he said as calmly as he could. 'I'll give you one hundred pesetas for it.'

The woman looked blankly at him.

'This –' he pointed at the typewriter – 'for this.' He showed her the money.

The lady shook her head vigorously.

'All right, two hundred,' he said, knowing it would still be a steal at a thousand.

'No,' the lady said.

'Fine,' Richmond replied. 'What do you want for it?'

'Not for sale,' the woman said, in hesitant English.

'Not for sale?' Richmond said incredulously. 'Then why the devil is it on display in your shop?'

At that moment Richmond had never wanted to own anything so much in his life. The feeling gripped him like a fever. He was sure that if this woman would not let him buy it from her, he would bash her over the head with it and run.

The woman seemed to notice the change in Richmond and shrugged.

'Five hundred,' she said.

'All right,' Richmond said, shakily removing the notes from his wallet, glad that the episode hadn't come to violence after all.

The rain had passed, and Richmond left the shop as quickly as he could, gripping the typewriter tightly and feeling dizzy with adrenalin. He ran up to his villa, stepped over his packed bags and put the typewriter on the desk.

Richmond typed the rest of that afternoon, all night and all of the following day. He missed his boat back to England. He

68

wrote until his fingertips were numb and he was faint from exhaustion. Finally, a week later, with the first few chapters done, he fell into bed and into a heavy, black sleep.

He awoke in the middle of the night, to the sound of tapping keys. He lurched out of bed and over to his desk.

His typewriter was typing quite unaided.

Richmond picked it up, turned it over and peered underneath. It must be some sort of trick, he thought. A joke typewriter that typed nonsense as a party trick. He tore out the page and read it. It was his voice – there was no question of that; the turn of phrase, the imagery, all exactly as he would have written them – picking up the story from where he had left it.

Richmond reeled back. Had he gone mad? Was he still asleep? A stub of his toe against his travelling trunk convinced him that he was indeed awake. Mad, then, he thought desperately and sat down on his bed.

The typewriter continued typing all through the night, with Richmond tearing out the pages as it went. This was good, he realised, extraordinarily good, better than anything he had written before. Then the fear started to give way to another emotion: excitement. This would be his masterpiece. This book would make him a millionaire. So what if its creation was supernatural? Wasn't every creative endeavour magical in some way?

He watched as the typewriter tapped steadily away, reading each page with mounting exhilaration. The plot spun its way to a climax that had Richmond weeping with joy, and a final sentence that would have the authors of London on their knees with envy.

Richmond sat back and giggled as the typewriter typed out THE END with a rhythmic flourish, then the keys were still. He gathered up the pages and tied them with a green, velvet ribbon. The Shipping Forecast by Antony Richmond adorned the title page in the typewriter's sinuous font.

As Richmond was slotting the manuscript into his leather case, the typewriter let out a little burst and then stopped again. Richmond approached it.

In the middle of a new page, in capital letters, was written:

PAYMENT PLEASE

Richmond studied it, confused. Payment? What did it mean? There was no coin slot, he was sure of that. Perhaps it was Zezia's little joke, or the maker's, at any rate. Richmond added the paper to his case and promptly forgot it, swept away by fantasies of his new life as Britain's greatest living novelist. That show-off Graham Greene would be 'green' indeed, Richmond chuckled to himself.

Richmond travelled back to London, with the typewriter hugged close to his chest, refusing to put it down even at meal-times. He didn't mind the stares. He thought the whole thing lent him an appropriately writerly eccentricity.

The response in London was better than that of his wildest dreams. His publisher suffered a heart attack while reading it and had to be replaced by his son, a news story that created a frenzy before the book had even been printed. And though most of his old writer friends stopped speaking to him because they were so sick with jealousy, Richmond didn't care, because his new friends were movie stars and jazz singers and members of the royal family.

But one night, following an enormous party at his new house in Eaton Square, Richmond awoke in the middle of the night to the sound of typing. Bleary-eyed, he walked over to Zezia and pulled out the paper.

PAYMENT PLEASE

Richmond looked at the familiar words and for the first time in a while, he felt rather queasy. He screwed up the page and eventually fell back to sleep.

Richmond's publisher began to ask what the next book would be, as did his new friends, and although he teased them that it was going to be his greatest work yet, Richmond hadn't a single idea of where to begin. The old fog had descended on his brain, and the Zezia typewriter hadn't typed a thing except PAYMENT PLEASE since it had finished The Shipping Forecast.

If he was honest with himself, the whole thing was beginning to make him uneasy. Then one night he awoke to the sound of the keys hammering even more loudly than usual. He had moved the typewriter to his dressing room, but the pounding still carried through the door. He approached Zezia tentatively; there were leaves of paper all over the floor, each of them covered in the same two words:

71

PAYMENT PLEASE PAYMENT PLEASE

Richmond had trouble sleeping after that.

His publisher insisted that he see some of Richmond's new book, and Richmond was forced to admit that he had nothing to show.

'Right,' said his publisher, 'I'm sending you away. You've been living it up in London for far too long. You need to clear your head.'

Richmond's publisher suggested a place called Shiverton Hall. He had been at school there and guaranteed that there wasn't a place on earth further away from everything. He'd have a word with the headmaster, and see if Richmond couldn't stay there while the place was empty for the summer holidays.

'No luxury. No distractions. Two months should break the back of it, wouldn't you say?' the publisher said.

Richmond couldn't argue. Perhaps he did need to be away from it all. Maybe Zezia would be better behaved when he had time to spend with her.

He took a train to Grimstone station, and the school groundsman picked him up in an ancient automobile.

'The headmaster's on holiday in Exmoor,' the grounds-man said as the car pulled up to the menacing bulk of Shiverton Hall. 'He'll be back in two weeks. If you need me I'm in the groundsman's cottage, about a mile from here.'

Richmond got out of the car, holding Zezia and a small bag.

'Where do I sleep?' he asked.

The groundsman shrugged. 'It's a school. Take your pick of the dormitories.'

The car sputtered off, leaving Richmond, cursing his publisher, to enter the hall alone.

Richmond soon found a perfectly nice room for himself, painted blue and with only one bed in it, and he began to unpack. No sooner had he put his typewriter on the table than it started up again with its plea.

PAYMENT PLEASE

'Right,' Richmond said to himself, sitting down at the small desk, his knees barely fitting under it, 'I've had enough of this.' He began to type.

WHAT DO YOU WANT?

The typewriter was still for a moment, then started up again.

PAYMENT PLEASE

Richmond typed back.

WHAT TYPE OF PAYMENT?

The typewriter answered: YOU.

The little bell on the typewriter sounded. Richmond stared at the paper. He typed slowly.

WHAT DO YOU MEAN, 'ME'?

YOU, *the typewriter answered.* PAYMENT PLEASE.

It was almost dark outside, and Richmond was beginning to regret coming out to this strange place. Regret was not a strong enough word.

He went downstairs and made himself a cup of tea in the small kitchenette that must have been used by the older boys to make toast during term time. Richmond walked over to the library, and looked for something comforting to read. There was a brightly coloured book of nursery rhymes on one of the side tables: that would do to steady his nerves. He lit a small fire in the grate, and began to read.

He was halfway through 'Oranges and Lemons' when he heard, from the floor above, echoing down the stairs and across the corridor, the faint sound of tapping.

Richmond tore up the stairs. He no longer cared what Zezia could do for him; he hated the thing, he didn't want it, he would throw it out of the window and that would be that.

He opened the door to his room and grabbed hold of the typewriter. He felt cold when he saw what it was writing.

Oranges and lemons,
Say the bells of St Clement's.
You owe me five farthings,
Say the bells of St Martin's.

When will you pay me?
Say the bells of Old Bailey.
When I grow rich,
Say the bells of Shoreditch.
Here comes a candle to light you to bed,
Here comes a chopper to chop off your head.
CHOP CHOP CHOP CHOP CHOP CHOP CHOP
CHOP CHOP CHOP CHOP CHOP CHOP CHOP
CHOP CHOP CHOP CHOP CHOP CHOP CHOP
CHOP CHOP CHOP CHOP CHOP CHOP CHOP
CHOP CHOP CHOP CHOP CHOP CHOP CHOP

Behind the sound of the keys was another sound, in the corridor, coming closer and closer to his room. A methodical thud, like an axe through wood.

Richmond's fear had reached a maniacal pitch. He opened the window, and held the typewriter out of it, but the thudding continued.

DON'T, *it typed.*

Richmond, panicking now, put it back on his desk and typed madly, his fingers fumbling on the keys.

HOW DO I PAY YOU?

The typewriter answered immediately: YOU.

Richmond began to type. He started with his parents, and his brother who had died at birth; he went on to his school days and the bully who had made his life a misery. Soon he was typing without even thinking; every secret, every petty cruelty he had ever committed, was laid bare on the cold whiteness of Zezia's paper.

The noise in the corridor had stopped, but Richmond was more concerned about what his hands were doing. They were moving quite independently of his brain, moving through university, through his first love, through the terrible way he treated her, past his first book.

He wanted to stop, but his hands continued, fingers blistering on the mother-of-pearl keys. Richmond began to feel faint, as though he himself were being pulled into the workings of the machine, becoming entangled in its oily cogs.

Was that the dawn he saw in the distance? Or the gleam of Zezia's silver ribbon spool? He could not tell.

The following morning the groundsman went into the hall to deliver some groceries to Mr Richmond.

He looked everywhere but could not find him; his room was empty, except for a finished manuscript tied with a green, velvet ribbon on the desk.

PAID IN FULL
by Antony Richmond

'No one ever saw poor Antony again,' Mrs Todd said sadly. 'Of course, *Paid in Full*, his autobiography, was an enormous success. So raw, so truthful. And of course, no one believed the bit at the end about the magic typewriter. Except for me.'

'Why did you believe it?' Arthur asked.

'Because I've lived near Shiverton Hall my whole life,' Mrs Todd replied. 'And far, far stranger things than that happen there. You'll see.'

She cocked her head and looked at Arthur. 'Or perhaps you already have?' she said quietly.

Arthur looked at the cherub-encrusted clock on the mantelpiece.

'Oh! It's already five,' he said, jumping up. 'I'll miss the bus.'

Mrs Todd got up and showed him to the door.

'Thank you,' she said. 'It's jolly nice to have someone to talk to. My children hardly ever come to see me nowadays. Busy.' She shrugged.

'It was nice talking to you too. I'm going to have to bring my friend George one day – he'll go crazy for that typewriter story.'

'Oh good! Well, I have plenty more where that came from. One of the benefits of being five hundred years old!'

'See you next week, Mrs Todd,' Arthur said as he made his way towards the forest. 'Thanks for the cake!'

'See you next week, Albert!'

'Oh . . .' Arthur paused. 'Sorry, Mrs Todd, I should have said earlier. My name's actually Arthur.'

Mrs Todd clapped her hand over her mouth in horror.

'Don't worry about it,' Arthur laughed. 'You'll just have to bake an even bigger cake next week to make up for it.'

Mrs Todd shook her head and laughed, then she disappeared into her miniature house, all of the bells and ribbons tinkling in the trees around her.

CHAPTER SIX

Arthur hit the high street just in time to see George limp towards him, his curly hair plastered to his sweaty forehead.

'Football went well, then?' Arthur giggled.

'I'm going to die,' George spluttered. 'Those eight-year-olds, they're vicious.'

'How were the Forge triplets?'

'Even worse,' George replied. 'Awarded the teams extra goals for kicking the ball at my head. They are pretty interested in you, though. Dan kept on asking me all sorts of questions.'

'Uh-oh. You don't think they're planning something, do you?'

'Well, it's either that or they've suddenly become your biggest fans.'

'So I'm in trouble.'

'I'd say so, yep,' George said cheerily. 'I might pop into Aunt Bessie's while we wait for the bus. Wanna come?'

'No way. I am not going in there for a second time,' Arthur said. 'She's trying to shift the bonbons again – be on your guard.'

George loped towards the cigar-scented fog of Aunt Bessie's and Arthur waited by the bus stop. Grimstone high street always looked like the sort of place you'd put on a poster to promote British tourism, with its pretty mismatched cottages and tea rooms, but Arthur particularly liked it at this time, in the evening, when the lights twinkled from the windows and mist hung over the cobblestones. It seemed rather more deserted than usual, though; in fact, once George had disappeared into the sweet shop Arthur seemed to be the only one around.

It was getting colder and Arthur pulled his wool blazer closer to him. He wasn't sure if it was the grey light of the evening or the sudden chill, but he had the uneasy feeling that someone was watching him. He looked behind him: nothing. When he turned back around, he jumped. There was a woman standing in front of him, rail-thin and haggard, wearing a thin nightdress, her long hair hanging over her face.

She sprang forward and clutched at Arthur's lapels.

Arthur struggled to get away, but her grip was surprisingly strong.

'Have you seen my son?' she whispered, her bloodshot eyes only a few centimetres from Arthur's. 'Have you seen my son?'

Arthur shook his head.

'He should be around here somewhere,' the woman said, letting go of Arthur and looking desperately down the empty road.

'I'm sorry,' Arthur replied. 'I haven't seen anyone. What does he look like?'

The woman looked at Arthur as if he were mad.

'You know what he looks like,' the woman hissed. 'His picture's all over town.'

Arthur realised who this woman was and took her arm gently. 'It's rather cold out here tonight,' he said, shrugging off his jacket and putting it over her shoulders. 'Would you like me to call someone for you?'

'My son,' the woman said miserably.

Arthur did not know how to reply.

The bell of Aunt Bessie's Sweet Shop rang out into the street and George emerged. The woman turned to Arthur and grabbed his hand.

'When you see him,' she whispered imploringly, 'tell him I'm looking for him.'

The woman scuttled away, nearly knocking George over and tipping his bags of bonbons on to the street.

'New girlfriend?' George laughed, looking after the woman as she disappeared down a side street. 'Looks like she's nabbed your blazer.'

'I think she's Andrew Farnham's mother,' Arthur said.

'Oh.' George's smile vanished. 'That's terrible. What did she say?'

'Nothing. Just looking for her son, I guess.' Arthur shivered. 'Another detention for me from Long-Pitt for losing my blazer,' he said grimly.

'You can have my spare one,' George said.

'Thanks, mate,' Arthur replied, hugely grateful. He knew his mum wouldn't be able to afford another one. For some reason, the Shiverton uniform cost as much as a handmade Italian suit.

George looked back down the street. 'Wait –' he squinted – 'is that Xanthe and Penny?'

The two girls were walking down the street towards them, their heads bent together conspiratorially.

'I thought they were working on the school paper. What are they doing here?' Arthur asked as they approached.

'Hey, guys,' Penny said as they reached the boys. 'Good afternoon?'

'What have you been doing in Grimstone?' George asked.

'Oooh,' Penny replied excitedly. 'We've been –'

'Shhhhh!' Xanthe said. 'Remember what Chuk said?'

'Oh right, yeah,' Penny said. 'Sorry, boys. Top-secret *Whisper* business, I'm afraid.'

'What? Not fair!' George whinged. 'What kind of top-secret business?'

'The secret kind,' Xanthe replied.

They chatted on the bus on the way back to Grimstone. The Forges had insisted on sitting near Arthur again, and he kept turning round to check that they weren't doing anything suspicious; every time he was met with the same maniacal grinning.

George was insanely jealous of Arthur's WAA. 'How come you get to just sit around eating and hearing awesome stories and I get repeatedly kicked in the trousers by a bunch of demon-children?'

George and the others absolutely loved Mrs Todd's typewriter story. 'It's not in any of Grandpa's books, you know. He's going to be so pleased when he hears it,' George said, rubbing his hands with anticipation. He was always trying – and failing – to impress his crotchety old grandfather.

When they got off the bus, Chuk was waiting in Shiverton's grand hall. Penny and Xanthe scurried over to him.

'Oh, I see why they're suddenly so interested in the school paper!' Arthur laughed, as he clocked Chuk flirting shamelessly with the girls.

'He's not even that good-looking!' George said huffily. 'I mean, yeah, OK, if you like that generic kind of tall, dark and handsome millionaire look then I suppose technically he's all right.'

'What do you think they're talking about?' Arthur asked.

'Let's walk past subtly and see if we can hear anything,' George answered.

The boys casually sauntered across the hall, pretending to take in its architectural features. George squinted up at the enormous chandelier and Arthur peered at the weaponry on the walls as they got closer to Chuk and the girls.

'Did you do it?' Chuk whispered.

'We couldn't,' Penny replied quietly. 'But I think next week we'll –'

She stopped and looked at the boys.

'I know what you're doing, George,' Penny sighed, as George pretended to inspect a candlestick on a nearby table.

'What?' George said innocently. 'I was just checking the . . . er . . . silver heritage of this . . . erm . . .'

'It's a candlestick, George,' Xanthe finished.

'Yes, exactly, candlestick,' George said.

'Right. Shall we go up to the *Whisper* office?' Chuk said.

'Yes,' Xanthe said, with a smug smile directed at Arthur. 'I think we need a bit of privacy.'

Penny, Xanthe and Chuk disappeared up the gigantic staircase, whispering as they went.

'What on earth are they up to?' Arthur asked as he and George watched them go.

'I don't know,' George said, 'but I hope it has something to do with my most recent cartoon. It's called "School Lasagne: Part II".'

CHAPTER SEVEN

Cornwall was looking even more dishevelled than usual. Today he was wearing an outfit that would not have looked out of place in a budget Seventies music video and was swigging from a bottle of cola, the contents of which were suspiciously clear.

'Bet you a quid that isn't water,' George whispered to Arthur as they settled into their seats. They were not in the art block; instead, Cornwall had decided to take the class on an 'Artistic Journey Around Shiverton Hall'. The class had already looked at the bloodthirsty murals on the dining-hall walls, the depressing mermaid statue in the middle of the fountain, and a stained-glass window entitled *Hell*, which depicted Shiverton Hall in spring.

The final leg of their tour was the Shiverton library and the Gainsborough painting that now hung above the fireplace. The portrait had caused quite a stir, with the students already speculating that it was most probably worth more than the entire Shiverton Hall estate put together.

Jake sat on the chair nearest to Cornwall, craning forward earnestly. 'All right, keen-o?' Penny said as she sat down beside him.

'Shhhhh,' Jake hissed. 'He's about to talk.'

Penny rolled her eyes at George and Arthur.

'Right,' Cornwall made a start, 'is everyone sitting comfortably? Then let's begin.'

He pointed to the portrait, which depicted a man and a woman, in liquid, dove-grey silks, sitting in the foreground of a vast, grassy landscape.

'This is Mr and Mrs Pontefract,' Cornwall began, squinting up at the painting. 'A hugely rich landowner and his equally loaded wife. This portrait was painted to commemorate their marriage, and to remind anyone who happened to walk past it quite how powerful they were. Everything you can see, from this lake to the left to the hills and forest in the distance, forms part of the Pontefracts' gigantic estate.'

George whistled.

'Impressive stuff,' Cornwall agreed. 'And this painting is one of Gainsborough's finest. As you can see, Mr Pontefract is holding a book. He was keen to be seen as a learned man, and not just a farmer, which the fashionable set of the day seemed to think he was. His wife's hands and lap are unpainted – does anyone have a guess as to why that might be?'

The class stared back at him blankly.

'The couple wanted Gainsborough to add a child as soon they had one, but sadly, it was not to be. The Pontefracts' only child disappeared a few months after she was born. Snatched from her nursery, where the painting was hanging.'

Penny looked at the blank space on Mrs Pontefract's lap sadly. 'How awful,' she said out loud.

'It is awful,' Cornwall agreed, 'and I'm afraid poor Mrs Pontefract didn't live much longer herself. When she died, Mr Pontefract gave the painting away. Said he couldn't bear to look at it.'

'I don't like it,' Xanthe said, screwing up her nose. 'It gives me the creeps.'

Cornwall looked at Xanthe with interest. 'That's unusually perceptive of you, Xanthe,' Cornwall replied. 'What makes you say that?'

The class turned to look at Xanthe. It was unlike her to be moved by anything, much less scared.

'I don't know,' she replied, looking uneasily at the painting. 'I just don't like it, that's all.'

Cornwall smiled and pointed up at the portrait. 'Xanthe isn't the first to be unnerved by this picture. Tell me, does anyone notice anything unusual about it?'

The students peered up at the painting.

'The faces . . .' Jake said suddenly.

'Good!' Cornwall responded. 'What about the faces?'

'They look . . . scared,' Jake said.

'Indeed they do. Difficult to perceive at first, but the longer you look, the more evident it becomes.'

Arthur noticed it for the first time, a slight tension in Mr Pontefract's mouth and a glimmer of fear in his wife's eyes. They seemed to be staring out of the painting imploringly, begging the viewer for something, but for what exactly was not clear.

'There is something else,' Cornwall continued. 'Something even stranger. Can anyone tell me what it is?'

The students searched the painting, but no one raised their hand.

'Look at the hill, just before the forest,' Cornwall said.

Arthur felt a ripple of anxiety when he saw what Cornwall was referring to. In fact, the whole class, one by one, began to shiver as they realised.

There was a figure standing on the hill.

Although it was barely more than a shadow, a dark whisper, its malevolence was somehow absolute. It seemed to be watching the couple, and in what must have been some painter's trick, the figure appeared to creep closer without ever actually moving.

'Gainsborough scholars call this figure "the Creeper", Cornwall said. 'What is odd about it, aside from the way it looks and the feeling it gives the viewer, is the fact that Gainsborough did not paint it. Or if he did, he painted it after he painted the rest of it. When the painting was completed and handed to the Pontefracts, Mrs Pontefract's younger sister made a watercolour copy in order to improve her brushstrokes. The copy is extremely detailed, and rather good, but it does not contain the figure.'

Cornwall plucked an old book from one of the shelves and opened it with a dusty crack. The volume contained a copy of the watercolour, and the students passed it round and examined it.

'So, where did it come from?' Cornwall continued. 'Who is the Creeper? Why did it appear? We only know that by the time the portrait was passed on to its next owner the Creeper was there.'

'Weird,' Penny said.

'It's not the only weird thing about this painting,' Cornwall said. 'According to various sources, this picture is cursed.'

'Great,' Arthur said under his breath. 'Exactly what this place needs.'

'Legend has it that in every place this portrait has hung, a child has disappeared,' Cornwall said. 'They say the Creeper clambers out of the painting and possesses the child . . . for whenever a child vanishes, so does the Creeper.'

The class looked nervously up at the picture. The figure seemed even more malevolent than before.

'If that's true then why hasn't someone just burned it?' Xanthe said sceptically.

Cornwall laughed. 'You'd be pretty idiotic to burn a painting that's worth a fortune. Curse or no!'

'Sir,' George said. 'Do you think it's a good idea that we have this painting here? You know, in a school full of kids.'

Cornwall smiled enigmatically and put on his sunglasses. 'Oh, I'm sure you'll all be all right,' he said. 'As long as the Creeper stays on that hill. It's when you can't see him that you should be worried.'

The bell rang, but the class remained, transfixed by the painting.

'Well, go on, then,' Cornwall sighed. 'Shoo!'

The class began to gather up their things, gossiping excitedly about the Creeper.

Arthur and George approached Cornwall, who seemed to be engrossed in a text message on his crystal-encrusted phone.

'Mr Cornwall,' Arthur asked politely.

'What?' Cornwall snapped.

'Do you think that story is true, about the painting? It's just . . . things have happened here before,' Arthur continued nervously.

'A cursed painting?' Cornwall laughed. 'Come on, you boys are too old to believe that sort of thing!'

'So, it's not true?' George asked.

Cornwall sighed and put his phone down. 'Look, half of Hampton Court is supposed to be haunted,' he said. 'There must be hundreds of old jugs or pictures or bits of furniture that are supposed to have weird properties. Are there stories about this painting? Yes. Does that mean I believe them? Of course not! I'm sorry to disappoint you, but it's only a story.'

'Yeah,' George muttered to Arthur as they left the library. 'I've heard that before.'

CHAPTER EIGHT

⁂

The following Wednesday, Arthur made his way up the path through the woods to Mrs Todd's house, trying not to think about the long fingernail that had been embedded in the trees so many centuries before.

It was a warm afternoon, and even though the woods glimmered in the sunlight, Arthur still felt a little anxious walking through them alone. Ever since the burned man had paid him the midnight visit at Christmas, Arthur was terrified that he might bump into him again.

Arthur paused. A twig snapped behind him. He turned around, but saw nothing, although, he realised uneasily, there were plenty of places to hide. He began to walk more quickly. He could see the smoke curling from Mrs Todd's chimney: he was nearly there. Something rustled in the bushes to his right and before he had time to run, he felt a hand on his shoulder.

He spun around, his fist instinctively clenched beside him, only to find George panting in front of him.

'George!' Arthur yelled. 'You nearly gave me a heart attack! What are you doing?'

'Sorry, Arthur,' George replied. 'I tried to catch up with you but you were absolutely pacing it. The Forge triplets gave me the afternoon off, said I was a worse player than the children and that I should "keep an eye" on you.'

'What does that mean?'

'Beats me. But I didn't stick around to ask. Do you think Mrs Todd would have a spare slice of cake for me?'

Mrs Todd not only had an extra slice of cake, but also seemed to have purchased the entire cake shop.

'I recognise you,' she said to George as she showed them into her cluttered sitting room. 'Have I met you before?'

'Nope,' George replied, his face already stuffed with a jam tart.

'Was your father at the school?' she asked.

'Yup, and my grandfather,' George said, moving on to a fondant fancy.

'That must be it,' she replied. 'I've lived here all my life. I think I must have seen every single student that ever passed through Shiverton Hall. Though I've no idea why parents would send their children there. A horrible place.'

'I told George your typewriter story,' Arthur said, gulping down some strong, sweet tea poured from Mrs Todd's silver teapot.

'Did you?' Mrs Todd replied, pleased. 'I've got nothing but stories these days, that's the problem with being so ancient, you see.' She smiled sadly.

'Do you believe the stories?' Arthur asked. 'About Shiverton?'

Mrs Todd chuckled. 'I don't think that there is a single person who lives in this village who doubts the stories. Most of them have one or two of their own.'

'Do you know any more?' George asked excitedly, spraying crumbs all over Mrs Todd.

She discreetly wiped them away with a floral handkerchief.

'More than I could count,' Mrs Todd chuckled. 'But I couldn't possibly tell you . . . You wouldn't sleep.'

George shifted forward on the sofa eagerly.

'Oh, all right,' Mrs Todd said. 'Maybe just one.'

THE FAIR

*I*n the summer of 1962 a travelling fair rumbled into Grimstone in the middle of the night. The mayor, a rather pompous man with a lopsided blond wig, was astonished to wake up and find the normally subdued Grimstone high street filled with carousels and helter-skelters and coconut shies. A silver and black painted sign in the middle of the high street read, Malvolio and Violetta's Marvellous Fair – You'll never want to leave!

The mayor elbowed his way through the crowds of excited children towards the great striped tent that had been erected in the middle of the fair, and demanded that the strong man who guarded the door let him in. Inside, the mayor discovered a young woman, no more than twenty, in a glittering river-grey costume and a plumed, crystal headdress, sitting at a desk. The girl looked up at the mayor with enormous violet eyes and asked him what the matter was.

The mayor had always been rather awkward around beautiful women and stammered that he would like to see the manager of the fair, not yet realising that he was already speaking to her. Violetta simpered and batted her eyelashes, and before the mayor knew what was happening, he was standing outside the striped tent, clutching two free tickets to the Ferris wheel and blushing furiously. It seemed that the fair could stay in town for as long as it pleased.

The fair was nothing like an ordinary travelling fair. It seemed almost Victorian, with its wooden roller coaster and candlelit fun house. There was no pop music blasting from the rides; instead, an old organ cranked out ancient seaside tunes, and two elderly twin sisters, only a few feet tall and wearing doll's clothes, sang folk songs about love in a strange, high harmony.

The children of Grimstone adored the fair, and spent all of their pocket money on its heart-shaped tokens, but the adults of the town felt uneasy about it. Although it was terribly pretty, and everyone who worked there seemed very polite, there was something not quite right about it. Something that made them feel as though they were looking at it through one of the fun house's warped mirrors. After a day or two, some of the villagers approached the mayor about it, and suggested that it might be time for the fair to move on. The mayor would have absolutely none of it, and said huffily that the fair, and its beautiful manageress, could stay for as long as they liked.

The weeks went by, or some thought they were weeks: it was becoming increasingly difficult to tell. Since the fair had come to town, time seemed to have a different texture and feeling, so that it had become impossible to work out whether something had happened a minute, an hour or even a day ago. The children queued up at the booth and bought their tokens and went on the rides and consumed stick after stick of candyfloss. Should they be at school? parents wondered hazily. Or was it still the weekend?

The performances in the striped tent had taken on the quality of dreams, or nightmares. The contortionist knotted himself into impossible positions; the twins knitted closer and closer together until they appeared to fuse into a single, two-headed body; the horses and their acrobatic riders gnashed sharp, fanged teeth; and even Violetta, beautiful and shimmering on her trapeze began to look like a mermaid that had been out of the water too long, puckered and dry as she whirled around the ceiling.

There was dust everywhere too. In the clunking pipes of the organ and between the slats of the roller coaster. And was the candyfloss really candyfloss at all? It looked more like spider's webs than spun sugar. The parents squeezed their eyes shut, in the hope that things would seem clearer when they reopened them but every time they did, Grimstone seemed stranger than before.

The children were beginning to behave strangely too. They had stopped talking, stopped giggling, or even screaming on the rides. They queued up silently, sucking on their sticks of rock. Even the Shiverton Hall students, who were normally the most rambunctious in the village, had hollow eyes and sallow skin, their grey uniforms fraying slightly at the pockets.

One evening, how many days or weeks or months after the fair came to town, no one was sure, Violetta climbed up to the top of the Ferris wheel, her little, glittering shoes neatly navigating the creaking scaffold. She held up her hands for attention and the fair ground to a halt.

There was to be a special show that evening. A very special man had travelled from far away to visit them all; it was to be the final show before the fair moved to another town.

The town filed into the marquee and sat on the wooden benches. It seemed impossible that the whole of Grimstone could fit into one tent, but the grown-ups had long ago stopped thinking about what was possible and what was not. Once every spot was filled, the strong man sealed the tent and the lights went out.

In the middle of the ring, a single spotlight clunked on.

Within the beam of white light, stood a tiny, wizened man. He wore a suit of deep navy velvet that seemed at least two sizes too big for him and bejewelled, high-heeled shoes. He looked out at the audience and smiled.

Violetta, who had become so wrinkled that she had the appearance of a glittering walnut, staggered out from behind the scenes.

'The Great Malvolio requires two volunteers,' she called out hoarsely.

The audience stared back at her, dazed.

Malvolio leaned down and whispered into Violetta's ear and pointed to a plump boy in the audience.

'The Great Malvolio has chosen,' Violetta said, and walked over to the boy, pulling him up by his wrist.

'Do you like magic tricks, boy?' she asked.

The boy did not answer. He was as limp and docile as the rest of Grimstone, who looked as though their limbs had been stuffed with sawdust.

The strong man wheeled a magic box into the ring; it was about the size of a coffin and painted with gold and silver stars. Malvolio guided the child into the box.

'And now for our second volunteer,' Violetta said. 'What about a girl this time?'

Another box was wheeled on, this one decorated with flames and shimmering snowflakes.

'STOP!'

Malvolio looked out at the audience, surprised.

Violetta narrowed her bloodshot eyes. 'Who said that?' she hissed, looking out at the constellation of blank faces. 'Who dares interrupt the Great Malvolio?'

A little girl, a few rows from the back, stood up. She had the look of a sleepwalker who had awoken to find herself standing in the garden in the middle of the night. She blinked towards the lights, confused.

'I . . . I . . .' the girl stammered, 'I think you should . . . stop . . . I don't like this trick . . . I don't like this fair.' The girl's voice was gaining power as the panic began to rise up in her.

Violetta smiled. 'How marvellous! Please give our second volunteer a warm hand.'

The strong man walked into the audience and picked up the girl. She struggled and screamed, but the audience simply sat and watched.

Malvolio and the strong man forced the screaming girl into the second magic box and slammed the door shut, buckling the sides with relish. The audience clapped politely.

'And now,' Violetta cried, 'the Great Malvolio will perform his finest trick.'

The twins began to bang a drum as Malvolio and Violetta sank into the darkness at the back of the tent.

In the beam of the spotlight, smoke began to rise out of the seams of the magic boxes and snaked up towards the ceiling. The muffled screams of the girl grew louder as she kicked and clawed at her box, but her cries were drowned out by the sound of the twins' drum, which was growing to a burning crescendo.

Suddenly the drumming stopped, and the tent was filled with an expectant silence.

Violetta leapt back into the spotlight, as young and glittering and beautiful as she had been when the fair arrived.

'Voilà!' she called, throwing open the boxes. 'The Great Malvolio has made your children disappear!'

Indeed, the magic boxes held nothing but thin air. One or two audience members idly noticed the frantic claw marks on the lid of the smaller box, but smiled courteously and applauded the show.

Malvolio reappeared to take his bow. The tiny, old wizard that had stood before them a few moments earlier had transformed into a tall and strapping young man with a grin like an accordion.

'Thank you, ladies and gentlemen,' Violetta tinkled, as the boxes were wheeled off. 'We hope you have enjoyed our little fair. Come back soon.'

The following morning, the town rose, sleepy-eyed and thick-headed, as though they had woken from a thousand-year sleep. One by one they staggered out of their houses into the streets, but the fair was nowhere to be seen – not a single shard of toffee apple or splinter of wood could be found to show that it had ever been in town. People were astonished to see the date on their newspapers and discover that only a day had passed since the fair had arrived. Many began to question whether it was all a mass delusion. A few people blamed the chemical plant a few miles away; perhaps it had poisoned the air?

That was until they heard about the missing children. A boy and a girl. A few townspeople had a nagging recollection . . . a boy and a girl . . . but they could not quite grasp the memory. Others vaguely remembered a glittering spotlight or the shape of a silver moon, but the memory seemed as far away and unreachable as the moon itself.

'What had happened to them?' Arthur asked.

Mrs Todd shrugged. 'What happens to any of the children who go missing from these parts?'

'What happened to the fair?' George said.

'Like all fairs, it moved on,' Mrs Todd replied. 'There are folk tales about it but nobody who claims to have seen it can ever remember enough about it. I remember more than most, but, who would believe me?'

'But why wouldn't they believe you? If children go missing from every town the fair visits? That's proof!' Arthur said.

'Thousands of children go missing every year, Arthur,' she said. 'And no one does a thing. They aren't all runaways.'

'Cheerful thought!' George said.

'Oh, I'm sorry!' Mrs Todd said. 'Look at me, rambling on! You've got an hour yet. Why don't you two nip off early and have a hot chocolate in town? You don't want to spend all afternoon with a shrivelled prune like me telling old wives' tales!'

'I do!' George said. 'I mean . . . not that you're a prune . . . er . . . you're a very beautiful . . . er . . .'

'Wrap it up!' Arthur said under his breath.

'It's all right,' Mrs Todd laughed. 'I am a prune, and rather a tired one at that. I could do with a rest. You two slip off and the ghastly Long-Pitt will never be any the wiser.'

'She is the coolest,' George said, as they wound their way through the woods towards Grimstone. 'If she was a million years younger . . .'

'Ha! I thought you'd like her!'

'Cake, horror stories . . . what's not to like?' George said.

The boys walked down Grimstone high street, and were just about to turn into Lily's Tea Rooms when they spotted two figures scuttling down the street.

'Wait . . .' Arthur said. 'Is that Penny and Xanthe?'

They peered at the hooded figures. It would have been a flawless disguise, were it not for the fact that Xanthe's beaded pigtails were sticking out from either side of her hood.

'What are they doing?' George asked. 'Shouldn't they be making moony faces at Chuk back at Shiverton?'

'Come on,' Arthur said, pulling his scarf around his face. 'Let's follow them.'

The girls hastened down the high street, and turned down one of the little cobbled alleys. Arthur and George tiptoed behind them, with George occasionally swinging into a doorway dramatically.

'You're not a spy, George,' Arthur whispered.

'I might be one day!' George said huffily.

The girls approached a thatched cottage. The garden looked as though it needed some attention, the grass was patchy and overgrown, bags of rubbish had been left in the flower beds and old crisp packets were tangled up in the rose bushes.

Penny and Xanthe navigated their way up the path, stepping over rotting food and dog mess. George and Arthur crouched behind the cottage gate and watched as Penny rang the doorbell. The door didn't open, so she tried again.

'There's no one here,' Penny said to Xanthe. 'Let's go.'

'Who are you looking for?' Arthur asked, standing up.

Penny and Xanthe jumped.

'For goodness' sake! What are you doing following us?' Penny said.

'Whose house is this?' Arthur asked.

'Hey, I recognise this place from the papers,' George said suddenly. 'This is Andrew Farnham's house.'

'What? The boy who went missing?' Arthur said. 'Why are you . . . ?'

Xanthe shrugged.

'Wait,' Arthur said. 'This doesn't have anything to do with *The Whisper*, does it? Please tell me that you are not here to interview that kid's mother?'

'We –' Xanthe began.

'Do you know what it feels like to have papers following you around, trying to pry into your family's life?' Arthur asked.

Penny and Xanthe glanced at each other guiltily. After the incident at Arthur's last school, his family had been in the papers daily.

'Well, I do! It feels bloody terrible,' Arthur continued hotly.

Penny looked as though she might burst into tears. Even Xanthe looked a bit embarrassed.

'Chuk thought that we might be able to find something out,' Penny explained. 'The police have no idea what happened and everyone else seems to have given up on it. Chuk suggested that since we're nearly the same age as Andrew we might notice something other people hadn't –'

'And if Chuk told you to set your hair on fire, would you do that too?' George said.

'Probably,' Xanthe admitted. 'He is incredibly handsome.'

Arthur rolled his eyes.

Suddenly, the front door opened, to reveal Mrs Farnham, barefoot and still wearing the nightdress Arthur had seen her in the week before.

'Who are you?' she asked.

'I'm so sorry, Mrs Farnham,' Arthur said. 'We were just going.'

'No, hold on,' Xanthe said. 'Mrs Farnham, we would like to ask you a few questions.'

'Xanthe!' Arthur shouted.

Xanthe shut her mouth sulkily.

'Wait,' Mrs Farnham said, looking at Arthur. 'I recognise you. You were the boy who gave me his jacket.'

'It's OK. Please don't worry about it,' Arthur replied, ushering the others down the path.

'No, no, please come in,' Mrs Farnham said, standing to one side. 'Let me get it for you.'

107

'We'd love to come in, thank you, Mrs Farnham,' Xanthe said.

'I didn't invite you,' Mrs Farnham snapped.

'Come on, Xanthe,' Penny said, guiding her away from the doorstep.

'We'll be at Lily's Tea Rooms, Arthur,' George called as Arthur was pulled into the darkness of the Farnham home.

The door slammed behind him. The house looked as empty and unkempt as Mrs Farnham herself. Flyers and leaflets bearing Andrew's face littered the floor.

'No use handing them out any more,' Mrs Farnham said. 'Everyone in town already has dozens of them.'

'I'm sorry, Mrs Farnham,' Arthur said quietly.

Mrs Farnham nodded, not, Arthur soon realised, as an affirmative gesture; it seemed more compulsive, as though she was counting the nods. Arthur waited for a few moments as she stared into the middle distance, her head bobbing up and down like something lost at sea.

'Come with me,' Mrs Farnham said suddenly. 'I know your jacket's somewhere.'

Mrs Farnham showed Arthur up the stairs, and Arthur felt more uncomfortable with every step he took. He wanted to leave, but Mrs Farnham had his hand tightly gripped in hers.

They walked along the landing and Mrs Farnham paused outside one of the bedrooms.

'That's my daughter Debbie's room,' she said. 'She and her father have gone to stay with my mum. They don't like to be in the house without him.'

'Are you going to join them?' Arthur asked.

'What if he comes back?' Mrs Farnham replied. 'And no one is here. He'll think we've forgotten him.'

Arthur nodded. They continued down the corridor, stepping over piles of newspapers bearing Andrew's name.

'That's Andrew's room,' Mrs Farnham said, gesturing towards it.

Andrew's room, unlike the rest of the house, was pristine.

'I clean it every day,' Mrs Farnham explained. 'For when he comes back.'

Mrs Farnham released Arthur's hand and wandered away, leaving Arthur standing awkwardly outside Andrew's room.

It was not unlike Arthur's own bedroom at home. The walls were covered in posters and photos, and every surface held a clutter of books and odd childhood knick-knacks that had not yet been thrown away. Andrew seemed keen on fossils, and had a little glass cabinet full of ammonites and broken pots.

Then Arthur spotted his jacket, in a crumpled heap on a chair.

'Mrs Farnham,' he called, 'I think I've found my jacket.'

He paused; there was no answer. He waited a few moments, and then walked over to the chair. As he picked up his blazer, he noticed something odd about Andrew's desk. It was a perfectly ordinary pine desk, but it was scratched to pieces. Arthur looked closer and realised that they were not just random scratches; someone had written on the desk. And it was the same word over and over again:

SCRACCHENSHODDEREN.

Arthur ran his fingers over the indentations, and his body gave an involuntary shudder that he felt deep in his bones.

'Someone walking over your grave?'

Arthur jumped. Mrs Farnham was standing in the doorway.

'Pardon?' Arthur said.

'When you have the shivers,' she said, 'they say someone is walking over your grave.'

'Right,' Arthur said, a little unsettled.

Mrs Farnham nodded towards the marks on the desk.

'He did that before he went,' she said.

'I'm so sorry,' Arthur said. 'I didn't mean to pry. I just saw my jacket in here.'

'Oh, there it is,' Mrs Farnham said hazily.

'You said he did this before he went,' Arthur said. 'Do you know what it means?'

'No,' Mrs Farnham said. 'It was from the book.'

'The book? What book?' Arthur asked.

'The old book he found up at Shiverton Hall. He shouldn't have taken it. I gave him a ticking off about it.

But boys will be boys,' she said quietly. 'I regret ticking him off now.'

'Do you know where the book is now?' Arthur asked.

'He gave it to Ronnie,' Mrs Farnham said. 'He was frightened of it, I don't know why. I had a look at it – it was only an old book.'

'Sorry, who is Ronnie?' Arthur asked.

'Ronnie Townsend,' Mrs Farnham replied. 'Lives across the road.'

A few minutes later, Arthur found himself knocking on the Townsends' door. A boy his age opened it; he had the same air of exhaustion and sadness that Mrs Farnham did.

'Are you Ronnie?' Arthur asked.

'Yeah,' the boy replied.

'I'm sorry, but I was just wondering whether you had that book Andrew lent you?'

Ronnie tried to close the door.

'Please,' Arthur said, 'I think that book might have something to do with Andrew's disappearance.'

'Of course it does!' Ronnie hissed. 'Now I don't know who you are, or how you know about that book, but believe me you want nothing to do with it.'

'I know someone who might be able to work out what it is,' Arthur pleaded.

Ronnie looked sceptical.

'I'll give it back, I promise,' Arthur said.

'I don't want it,' Ronnie laughed bitterly. 'If you take it then I don't want it back.'

'OK, agreed,' Arthur said.

Ronnie opened the door fully and let Arthur in.

A woman leaned out of the kitchen.

'Who's this?' she asked jovially. 'One of your school friends?'

'Yes, Mum,' Ronnie mumbled, ushering Arthur upstairs.

'Is he staying for tea?' Ronnie's mum asked.

'No, Mum,' Ronnie yelled down.

He slammed his bedroom door and reached into his cupboard. At the back was a wooden box, fastened with a heavy padlock. He unlocked it and took out a package encased in a cocoon of Sellotape. Arthur looked at it quizzically. 'It was the only thing that stopped me from opening it.' Ronnie shrugged.

'What do you mean?' Arthur asked.

'Andrew begged me not to look in it but, well, put it this way, that's easier said than done,' Ronnie said, picking up the package with two fingers as though it was poisonous.

'Do you know what it is?' Arthur asked.

'No,' Ronnie said. 'All I know is that whatever was inside it made Andrew go completely nuts.'

'Nuts how?'

'He thought he was being followed – that someone was watching him.'

'And were they?'

Ronnie sighed. 'I never saw anything.'

'Do you really know someone who can help?' Ronnie asked quietly, as he showed Arthur back downstairs to the front door.

'I hope so,' Arthur replied.

Ronnie took a deep breath. 'Thank you.' Suddenly, something occurred to him. 'Sorry, I just realised I don't know your name,' he said, holding out his hand.

'Arthur Bannister.'

Ronnie stared at Arthur disbelievingly. 'Did you say Arthur Bannister?' he said slowly.

'Yes,' Arthur replied, confused. 'Why?'

'Then this book belongs to you,' Ronnie whispered.

'What do you mean?' Arthur asked.

Ronnie gave an odd laugh. 'We stole it from your pigeonhole.'

CHAPTER NINE

Arthur glanced around Toynbee's cluttered classroom. The chaotic collection of historical artefacts had been added to over Christmas. A monkey's paw in a velvet box now sat on the desk, and a rusting suit of armour stood awkwardly next to the Egyptian sarcophagus, as though they were on a date.

Toynbee examined the book with interest. 'He said it was put in your pidge?' he said.

'Yes.'

'By a hooded figure?'

Arthur nodded.

'Well, that doesn't sound good,' Toynbee said grimly.

Toynbee opened the drawer in his desk and retrieved a long, thin knife, with an elaborately bejewelled hilt.

'What is that?' Arthur asked.

'Oh, this?' Toynbee said, looking at the knife. 'Splendid, isn't it? It is rumoured to have belonged to Queen Nefertiti. I mostly use it to open letters.'

Toynbee began to cut away at the reams of Sellotape, until he revealed the book itself. He picked it up and sniffed it.

'It's certainly been burned a fair few times,' Toynbee said. 'It's an odd sort of book that doesn't burn, wouldn't you say?'

Arthur shifted nervously from foot to foot.

'What is it, Arthur?' Toynbee asked gently, peering at him over his gold-rimmed glasses.

'Someone paid me a visit in the holidays,' Arthur said.

'Someone . . . ?'

'A man wearing a hood,' Arthur said.

Toynbee put the book to one side. 'Where did you meet him?' he asked.

'He came to our flat, in the middle of the night. And . . .' Arthur stopped.

'And . . . ?'

Arthur bit his lip. 'He threatened me,' he replied. 'He told me not to come back to Shiverton Hall.'

'Do you have any idea who he was?'

'None,' Arthur said. 'But when he took off his hood . . .'

'Go on, Arthur,' Toynbee said softly.

'His whole face was scarred. It looked like he had been in a fire,' Arthur whispered.

Toynbee considered this for a moment. 'And you think this man may have been the one who put this book in your pidge?' he asked.

'Well, it would make sense,' Arthur said. 'Ronnie said the figure was wearing a hood, and the book is burned.'

Toynbee nodded. 'It does seem like a reasonable hypothesis,' he agreed.

'Sir,' Arthur said, 'I can't help thinking that this is all my fault – Andrew going missing. That book was meant for me. I should never have come back here.'

'Arthur,' Toynbee said kindly, 'it is not your fault. You cannot blame yourself for this. Those boys were trespassing and took something that did not belong to them. What's more, we do not yet know that this book has anything to do with Andrew's disappearance.'

'Wouldn't it be safer for everyone if I left the school?' Arthur asked miserably.

'Of all the things this place may be,' Toynbee said, 'safe has never really been one of them, with or without your presence.'

'I just seem to attract disaster wherever I go,' said Arthur.

'You've not been lucky, I'll grant you that,' Toynbee chuckled. 'But you're a good boy, Arthur, and the good will always out.'

'I'm a Shiverton, though, aren't I? I can't be all good.'

'No one is all good,' Toynbee said quietly. 'Let me have a look at this book. Leave it with me. I promise you, if I find anything that might be a danger to you or any of the other students, I'll put you on the first train to London. You have my word.'

'All right,' Arthur agreed.

'Who have you told about all of this?'

'No one,' Arthur said. 'I came straight to you, and I haven't even told the others about the burned man – I didn't want them to worry.'

'I think you're right. There's no use in everyone panicking. Try to keep it to yourself if you can for the moment.'

'Yes, sir,' said Arthur.

'Oh, and Arthur?' Toynbee said, as Arthur was leaving.

'Yes?'

'Chin up.'

Arthur smiled and hurried away from Toynbee's classroom. Now that the book was out of his hands he felt two stone lighter; he almost wanted to skip back to house.

The grounds were completely deserted; prep would have already started. Arthur groaned as he remembered the maths homework that he had to hand in the following morning. At least the pages and pages of equations would take his mind off Andrew Farnham and his poor mother.

Suddenly, Arthur stopped. Someone was watching him. He looked around the empty grounds, but saw no one. Yet he felt, with absolute certainty, the uneasy sensation of eyes on his skin.

'Hello?' he called out. There was no response.

'Hello?' he called again.

Arthur felt something tug at his sleeve.

He yelped and looked down, but there was nothing there.

'Is someone there?' Arthur asked, his voice shaking.

He thought he heard laughter, or was it just the wind in the trees?

He wanted to bolt, but he had the feeling that he mustn't run, that whatever it was that was watching him wanted to play a game and would certainly chase him. He set off calmly towards Garnons, concentrating with all his might on steadily putting one foot in front of the other.

After a few steps, he knew he was right. The presence seemed to lose interest, and the feeling of being watched disappeared as quickly as it had come. Arthur shivered, and walked faster towards Garnons.

'Please!'

Arthur paused again. What was that? The voice came from within the maze.

Reluctantly he crept towards it, stepping over the flaking OUT OF BOUNDS sign that hung on a chain across the entrance.

'I'm doing everything I can,' the voice whispered frantically.

Arthur peeked around a corner of the maze, and was surprised to see Cornwall, his jewellery glinting in the moonlight. He was pacing up and down one of the pathways, biting his nails.

'I can't do it,' Cornwall said.

'It's too late for that now,' a voice hissed back.

Arthur craned his head a little further around the maze, but Cornwall's companion was too far in the shadows to be seen.

'There must be something else I can do,' Cornwall said desperately.

'Do you have any suggestions?' the voice replied. Arthur could hear the mockery in its tone.

'It's just . . . it's a school. It's not right,' Cornwall said.

The voice chuckled. 'You're wrong about that, Cornwall,' it replied. 'It's perfect.'

'I don't want to do it. I've changed my mind,' Cornwall cried.

A hand reached out of the shadows and grabbed Cornwall by the wrist. Cornwall whimpered.

'It's a little late to have a conscience now, don't you think?'

Cornwall nodded dumbly.

'Good,' the voice said. 'Run along now.'

Arthur darted out of the maze and along the path before Cornwall could see him.

He replayed the conversation back in his head as he hurried back to house.

It's a school, Cornwall had said. *It's not right.*

Arthur dared not think about what he meant.

CHAPTER TEN

Arthur relayed Cornwall's curious conversation to his friends in the school library the following morning.

'And did you see who he was talking to?' George asked.

'It was too dark,' Arthur replied.

'It doesn't sound that suspicious,' Jake said.

'No? Then why have a conversation in the maze in the pitch dark?' Arthur asked.

'Cornwall's eccentric.' Jake shrugged.

'You have to admit it does sound pretty dodgy,' Penny said.

'You think everything sounds dodgy,' Jake huffed. 'You know, I'd just like to get through one term at this place with no bloody intrigue or excitement.'

'Good luck with that, mate,' George said.

'Wait, look!' Penny whispered, nudging Arthur. Cornwall had wandered into the library. He looked a little sweaty and rather out of sorts.

'Hello, Mr Cornwall,' Jake called out.

Cornwall flinched. 'Oh,' he said, waving half-heartedly. 'Hello, Jake.'

Cornwall seemed to be eyeing up the Gainsborough painting, although he was pretending to read a book.

'What is he up to?' Arthur whispered.

'No idea,' George said. 'But the Creeper's still on the hill. So that's one less thing to worry about at least.'

Arthur looked up at the dark figure. 'For now,' he replied grimly.

That afternoon, Arthur and his friends stood on the concrete parade ground in the driving rain and waited as the Forge triplets screamed at them. CCF, the Combined Cadet Force, was mandatory for all second years, and training mostly constituted getting yelled at by Dan Forge while wearing army camouflage. Every Thursday they had to learn how to make a shelter, how to read a map, and how to shoot a gun. The whole thing culminated in a camping exercise at the end of the term.

Arthur quite enjoyed it, especially since the Forge triplets had inexplicably decided to be extra nice to him, although they did appear to be taking out whatever surplus aggression they had on George, who had been called every swear word in the dictionary, and even some new ones.

'Grant!' Dan Forge screamed. 'Pay attention or drop and give us fifty.'

George groaned. He had already given them ten and could barely feel his arms.

After doing what felt like a million star jumps, the students were split into groups, and Arthur, George, Jake, Penny and Xanthe collected their map and compass for orienteering. They clambered on to the school bus with the others, and were taken to a desolate stretch of land a few miles from the school.

'I hate CCF,' Penny grumbled.

They were supposed to find their way back to Shiverton Hall, but in spite of Jake and Xanthe's best efforts, George's appalling sense of direction and Penny's insistence that they avoid walking up any hills meant it wasn't long before they found themselves well and truly lost.

'Where are we?' Arthur asked, rain dripping into his eyes.

'I think . . .' Jake said, studying the map, 'that we're on Bone Hill.'

Bone Hill was so called, because it was the site of a medieval grave. It was also studded with pale rocks, which looked like crooked teeth jutting out of a skull.

'Brilliant!' George said. 'We get away from our haunted

122

school for five minutes and find our way on to an ancient burial ground. Top marks.'

Xanthe looked out at the grey landscape. 'How far are we, exactly?' she asked uneasily.

They peered through the haze of rain, but could not make out anything that could be Shiverton Hall.

'Wait,' Penny whispered. 'I see something.'

Her friends followed her eye line.

About a mile away, on the brow of the opposite hill, stood a figure. Even though it was barely more than a silhouette, the shape of it filled Arthur with lurching primordial dread.

'Maybe it's one of the Forges,' George said weakly.

'No, it isn't,' Arthur replied.

No one argued with him.

'We've got to run,' Penny whispered.

'You don't need to tell me twice,' George said.

They ran screaming through the rain, too terrified to turn back. They sprinted over the hills, hauling themselves over fences; even Penny, wheezing at the back, managed to keep up. Eventually the rain cleared enough to let them get their bearings and they limped back to the school, sodden, and shivering with cold and fright.

The Forge triplets asked where they'd been, since they hadn't ticked off any of their check points, and Dan Forge was even angrier than usual when they said they'd been lost.

'It's dangerous around here,' Dan sneered. 'And I don't rate any of your chances against Skinless Tom up on the hills. Especially not you –' he pointed at George – 'he'd wear your face as a hat.'

'We didn't do it on purpose!' Penny protested.

'Use the bloody map next time,' Dan said. 'Or I'll have you all stitching name labels into the first years' pants for the rest of the year.'

As they began to leave, Dan grabbed Arthur tightly by the arm and whispered in his ear threateningly, 'Be careful, Scholarship. We don't want something horrible happening to you, do we?'

Arthur shook Dan off, resisting the urge to flick one of his cauliflower ears, and he and his friends trudged back to their houses, their boots squelching as they went.

Back in the Garnons library, drying by the fire and with a cup of tea in his hand, Arthur took a deep breath.

'All right,' he said to George. 'Who on earth is Skinless Tom?'

George grinned. 'I was afraid you'd never ask.'

SKINLESS TOM

*L*izzie Compton was furious about moving to the middle of
nowhere. She and her family had lived in Liverpool her
whole life, but her mum had recently inherited a house near a
place called Grimstone, and since her dad had been laid off,
her parents had the bright idea of 'starting afresh'.

It was the summer of 1979, and Lizzie had been about to go
to secondary school with all her friends. She had not spoken to
her parents since the move was first discussed the month before.

'I'm not coming!' Lizzie had screamed, slamming her bedroom door shut. 'You can go without me!'

Unfortunately for Lizzie, her parents had refused to leave
her behind, and she found herself stuffed in the back of their
old Volvo surrounded by boxes of items that were too precious
to send in the van, with her grandfather's ashes in an urn on
her lap.

If there was any consolation, it was that her older sister, Susan, was even more miserable about the move than she was, and had spent the entire journey so far sobbing loudly, mascara running down her face.

'What is this place?' Susan wailed as they drove down Grimstone high street. 'It's so small! Where are all the shops?'

'There are shops, Susan, dear,' her father said patiently. 'Look, there's a fishing shop there, and a bookshop over there.'

'WHAT AM I SUPPOSED TO BUY IN A BOOK SHOP?' Susan screamed, collapsing into another gale of tears.

They drove through Grimstone and just as they emerged out into the countryside, they turned down a somewhat overgrown drive. Ahead of them, sitting on top of a hill, was their new house. It was much larger than the photographs had implied, more of a mansion than a house. Three storeys high and perfectly symmetrical, it was painted cream with duck-egg blue shutters.

'It's beautiful,' Lizzie breathed.

The Compton family stepped out of their car and looked up at their new home.

'It looks like a doll's house!' Mrs Compton said.

The house was even prettier inside, with delicate floral wallpaper and enormous sash windows that looked out over the hills.

'What do you think, girls?' Mr Compton asked.

'It's OK,' Susan sniffed.

126

The family started to settle in. Susan yelled until she got the bigger room on the first floor, with its own frilly dressing table, complete with a set of enamelled hairbrushes and mirrors. Lizzie was given the attic room, which – from the look of the rocking-horse wallpaper – had once been a nursery. As she and Susan had shared in Liverpool, Lizzie loved the fact that she had a bedroom all to herself, even if it was smaller. The novelty of privacy would take a long time to wear off.

Grimstone was only a twenty-minute walk away, and even though Susan had dubbed it 'The Most Boring Place in England', Lizzie rather liked it. A wonderful old lady ran Aunt Bessie's Sweet Shop and always gave Lizzie an extra lollipop when she stopped by. Lizzie didn't much care for Bessie's young daughter, though, or the way she stared at the customers accusingly while pretending to smoke a pack of candy cigarettes.

The other children in the village hadn't been terribly friendly; in fact, they hadn't said a word to Lizzie or her sister. Susan was extremely pretty, and was usually surrounded by admirers and girls wanting to borrow her coral lipstick. The lack of attention had made her even more unbearable than normal and Lizzie hoped that matters would improve once they started school.

They didn't. On their first day of school, they were completely ignored. When Lizzie was asked to introduce herself in front of her new class, the other students averted their eyes. At lunch she was forced to sit with her sister, because every time one of them tried to sit with a group, the other children would move silently to another table.

'What is going on?' Susan hissed. 'I'm the prettiest girl here by miles.'

Lizzie rolled her eyes.

'Why aren't they talking to us?' Susan continued. 'Probably intimidated, stupid country bumpkins.'

'And you're so nice too!' Lizzie said.

'I know!' Susan agreed, oblivious.

At the end of the day Susan stormed back to their house, while Lizzie walked through the town, with the intention of stopping by Aunt Bessie's.

'Pssst,' Lizzie heard.

She stopped.

'Psst!' someone said. 'Over here!'

Lizzie saw a small, bespectacled face peeping out from an alley. She walked over and found a short, chubby boy in a blue mackintosh, his hand thrust in a packet of crisps.

'Hi,' Lizzie said.

'Shhhhh,' the boy replied. 'I can't be seen talking to you.'

He pulled her into the alley, checking that no one was coming.

'Why not?' Lizzie said, outraged.

'It's nothing personal,' the boy replied. 'You and your sister, you live in the house on the hill, right?'

'Yes,' Lizzie said.

'You've got to move out,' the boy said.

'What do you mean?' Lizzie laughed. 'We've only just got here.'

'And you'll be leaving one way or another, you can be sure of that, so my advice is: do it now.'

'Why?' Lizzie said.

'Didn't you wonder why you moved in the first place?' the boy asked.

'Mum inherited it,' Lizzie said.

'Who from?'

'From an aunt.'

'And have you ever met this aunt?' the boy said, a touch of smugness in his voice.

'Well . . . no,' Lizzie admitted.

The boy sighed. 'I couldn't help but notice,' he said, 'that your sister is rather good-looking.'

Lizzie sighed. 'Look, if that is why you dragged me here then –'

'It isn't!' the boy replied. 'If you want to know, I actually think you're prettier, but that isn't the point. The point is that every few years, a family moves into that house, and they always have children our age, and one of them is always . . . attractive.'

'So?'

The boy glanced around and leaned towards Lizzie, lowering his voice.

'Have you ever heard of Skinless Tom?' he whispered.

'Skinless Tom?' Lizzie asked.

'Shhh!' the boy hissed. 'Keep your voice down when you say it. He's known as Skinless Tom around here, but in other places they call him Tommy Rawhead or Bloody Bones.'

'Who is he?'

The boy hesitated. He could hear the voices of a gang of schoolkids making their way through the town; he did not want to be caught talking to Lizzie.

'It doesn't matter who he is,' he said quickly. 'What matters is that you and your sister get out of that house.'

'But how could we –'

'I don't care! Beg, cry, burn the bleeding place down, it doesn't matter!'

The voices were getting closer and the boy was panicking.

'I have to go,' he said.

'Wait!' Lizzie said, grabbing him by his mackintosh sleeve. 'I don't believe you.'

'You're lucky I told you anything at all,' the boy hissed. 'If you love your sister, get out of that place.'

He yanked his sleeve free and scurried away.

'I don't love my sister,' Lizzie called after him. 'I don't even like her!'

Later, at dinner with her family, Lizzie decided to do some probing.

'Mum,' she said casually, 'what was your aunt like? The one who lived in this house?'

130

'Do you know,' her mother answered, 'I never met her. She was my great-aunt apparently, on my father's side.'

'Didn't you think it was odd? To inherit a house from a woman you'd never met?'

'I didn't think it was odd,' her mother answered. 'I thought it was too good to be true! You hear of these things happening but you never think they'll happen to you.'

'Well, I wish it hadn't,' Susan sulked. 'I hate it here.'

'Didn't you make any friends at school today, dear?' their father asked mildly, used to pacifying his eldest daughter.

'No,' Susan growled. 'Not that I'd want to be friends with any of them anyway.'

Lizzie decided to change the subject.

'Have you ever heard of Skinless Tom?' Lizzie asked her mother.

Mrs Compton chewed thoughtfully. 'Skinless Tom? No. Is he a boy at school?'

'Or Tommy Rawhead? Bloody Bones?' Lizzie pressed.

'Oh, Bloody Bones!' Mr Compton cried. 'I remember him! We used to terrify each other about Bloody Bones when we were at school. "Bloody Bones is creeping up the stairs". Do you remember that, dear?' he asked his wife.

'I hated all those horror stories.' Mrs Compton shuddered.

Mr Compton leaned in towards his two daughters. 'Legend has it that Bloody Bones was a teenage boy who worked in an abattoir. One evening, so the story goes, his shirt got caught up in one of the cogs. He screamed for help, but no one could hear him over the noise of the machines, and he was pulled in. When they found him, he was hanging up with the pigs and the cows, skinned alive.'

'DAD!' Susan yelled. 'I'm trying to eat!'

'The legend says that Bloody Bones is always looking for a child whose skin will fit him.'

'That's enough!' Mrs Compton said. 'Or none of us will sleep tonight.'

'But it's not true, is it?' Lizzie asked. 'It's just made up?'

'Of course it's made up. I heard pretty much the same story at my school,' Mrs Compton said.

'All stories have to start somewhere,' Mr Compton said in a spooky voice. 'Why not here?'

Later that night, Lizzie found that she couldn't sleep. The house creaked and rumbled and groaned, as most old houses will when listened to by a nervous child. She knew that the boy must have been teasing her, but it didn't stop her from seeing a glistening, bloody face every time she closed her eyes.

The following day at school, Lizzie sought out the boy. She went to the school secretary and described him, claiming that he had dropped a textbook in town the day before. The secretary thought for a moment. 'That sounds like Donald Stoker. Classroom 2b,' she said.

Lizzie waited outside the classroom and accosted Donald as he left for break.

'I'm not talking to you,' he said once he noticed her. 'Leave me alone.'

'I just wanted to ask you something,' Lizzie said.

'Look,' Donald said, glancing nervously at the other students in the corridor, 'we don't talk to the kids who live in that house, OK?'

'Why not?' Lizzie asked.

'Because they never last very long,' Donald sighed.

'So what can I do?' Lizzie asked.

'I told you what to do,' Donald replied. 'Get out of there.'

He pulled Lizzie closer to him and whispered, 'He lives inside your house.'

Lizzie made her father search the house a hundred times, and her mother said it served him right for scaring his daughter so much. No matter how many times her parents told her that it was just a story, Lizzie wouldn't believe them.

Matters deteriorated when Susan came tearing down the stairs one morning, claiming that when she had looked in her enamelled hand-mirror, a skinless, blood-soaked face had appeared in it. Mr Compton scolded her for teasing her sister, who was now completely frantic, insisting that they should leave the house immediately.

One Saturday evening, sick of their daughters' squabbling, Lizzie's parents decided to go out for a romantic dinner.

'Yuck!' Susan said.

'Thank you, Susan,' Mrs Compton said. 'Since you're old enough now you can look after your sister.'

133

'Shouldn't we get a babysitter, just in case?' Lizzie said nervously.

'It'll be good for you two to spend some quality time together,' Mr Compton reasoned.

Lizzie watched miserably as the tail lights of her parents' car disappeared down the drive.

'I'm going to be on the telephone in my room,' Susan said haughtily. 'Don't you dare listen in.'

After Susan had been upstairs for an hour, Lizzie crept over to the telephone and quietly picked up the receiver.

Susan was talking to her best friend, Carol, who had lived a few doors down from them in Liverpool.

'I never really liked him,' Lizzie heard Susan say over the crackling line.

'Yes, you did!' Carol scoffed.

'Wait,' Susan said. 'Did you hear a click? Lizzie! You'd better not be listening in!'

Lizzie held her breath.

'It's OK. I must have imagined it,' Susan said finally.

'I'm so jealous,' Carol said. 'It sounds so amazing. I can't believe you're the most popular girl at school already.'

Lizzie tried to muffle her giggles.

'It is pretty amazing,' Susan agreed blithely. Lizzie could tell from her sister's smug, faraway tone that she was admiring her face in the mirror – something she did for at least an hour a night.

'Do you have a boyfriend yet?' Carol asked excitedly.

Lizzie held her breath, wondering what lie her sister would come up with for an answer. Lizzie couldn't wait to torment Susan about it.

'Hang on,' Susan sighed. 'My annoying little sister is knocking on my bedroom door.'

Lizzie froze. She wasn't anywhere near Susan's room. She heard the knocking faint on the line and the sound of Susan laying the receiver down on her bed to open the door.

Before Lizzie had time to warn her sister she heard a scream. Lizzie sprinted up the stairs, but there was no one in the hall. She ran to Susan's room: it was empty. The receiver was still on the bed, and Lizzie could hear Carol's tinny voice calling her sister's name.

Susan was nowhere in the house. Lizzie called the restaurant and spoke to her parents.

When they arrived home their daughter was babbling, trying to explain what had happened. Mr Compton rushed around the house, searching in all of the rooms.

'She isn't here,' he said anxiously. 'I think we'd better call the police.'

'Wait!' Mrs Compton said, her voice flooded with relief. 'There she is! Whatever is she doing outside in the rain? Susan! Come back inside!'

Lizzie peered out of the window, through the heavy rain.

Susan was standing in their back garden, looking in at the house, clutching the hand-mirror in her left hand. Except Susan looked different, her beautiful face sagged around the

skull in a peculiar way, and her skin was baggy around the
arms, like a jumper that was too big.

'Mum,' *Lizzie whispered,* 'that isn't Susan.'

'That is the grossest thing I have ever heard,' Arthur said,
disgusted.

'They demolished the house after that,' George said.
'Now it's just an old story that Grimstone kids tell to scare
each other.'

'So you don't think it was Skinless Tom back there on
the hill, then?' Arthur asked, not really wanting to know
the answer.

'I hope not,' George said. 'I really don't fancy my face
being worn as a balaclava, do you?'

CHAPTER ELEVEN

Arthur felt certain that all of these things – Andrew Farnham's disappearance, the burned book, the Creeper, the hooded man that had appeared at his house in the middle of the night and Cornwall's mysterious conversation – must be linked. He lay awake at night thinking about them, but he could see no obvious connection.

There was something else that kept him awake too. He increasingly felt as though he was being watched, monitored, like a deer in a hunter's cross hairs. Occasionally he would feel a tap on his shoulder, or another tug at his sleeve, or something grasping at his hand at night, but when he turned to look, he would find nothing there at all.

It was half-term soon, but he was almost as anxious about going home as he was about staying at Shiverton

Hall. He certainly didn't want to see the burned man again, especially since he had ignored his warning. Arthur wondered whether it might have been wiser to listen to the stranger, no matter how frightening he looked.

Arthur ran over everything again as he made his way to Cornwall's class, but nothing seemed to make sense. He was starting to suspect that it was no coincidence that a boy had gone missing after the arrival of the Gainsborough, with its strange creeping figure. Arthur had to remind himself once again that, since the Creeper had not moved from the painting, he was worrying over nothing, just another scary Shiverton story.

The lesson began with Cornwall sitting at his desk, staring into space, his left eye twitching. The teacher's behaviour had become increasingly eccentric since the night in the maze. He appeared to have given up teaching entirely, and now merely sat and glowered at them all during lessons. And as the weeks went by, his hair grew straggly, his velvet outfits a little worn, and his mood edgy and irrational. Even Jake had started to worry that Cornwall might be a little unhinged.

'Right,' Cornwall said, once Arthur had taken his seat, 'I've been ticked off by Long-Pitt for not teaching you the correct syllabus.'

'Finally,' Xanthe muttered.

'Out!' Cornwall said, pointing to the door.

'What? Again?' Xanthe cried.

'Maybe it'll teach you some manners,' he said.

Xanthe grumblingly gathered up her things and stalked out.

'Now, just so you know,' Cornwall continued, 'I have no intention of teaching you the syllabus. Art isn't on a syllabus. If you want to learn the "syllabus" then you can go read a book.'

'What about our exams?' Penny asked.

'Exams are a waste of time,' Cornwall replied haughtily. 'I never passed an exam in my life and look at me now.'

The class looked at him dubiously. He seemed to have some chewing gum stuck to his shirt.

'What I want you to do today,' Cornwall said, 'is to begin a self-portrait. It can be in any medium – oil, charcoal, gouache or clay . . . whatever you like. You will have until the end of this term to complete it.'

'Will it go towards our coursework?' one of the students asked.

'What's coursework?' Cornwall's expression was blank.

'Well, it looks like we're all failing our art exams,' Penny whispered.

She needn't have bothered to keep her voice down, because Cornwall had already put his head on his desk and fallen asleep.

'What is up with him?' Arthur asked.

'He's losing it,' Penny said. 'Some of the third years caught him crying in the library.'

'What?' Arthur said.

'He's snapped,' George said.

'He doesn't seem to be very . . . engaged, does he?' Jake admitted, looking at Cornwall's slumped form.

'Why did he even agree to take this job in the first place?' George said.

'That,' Arthur replied, 'is a very good question.'

When Penny and Xanthe went into the *Whisper* offices that Wednesday afternoon, they had a plan. Chuk was editing a criminally boring article about greenfly in the school rose garden when they burst in.

'Hello, you two,' Chuk said. 'You're early.'

As usual, it took the girls a moment to adjust to being in Chuk's presence, and they spent the first few minutes rambling about the weather and trying not to fall over.

Once Penny had pulled herself together enough to put one word in front of another, she disclosed the purpose of their visit.

'What do you know about Inigo Cornwall?' Penny asked.

Chuk put his pen down and leaned back in his chair. 'I tried to interview him for *The Whisper* when he arrived,' he said, 'but he told me in pretty strong terms that he doesn't speak to the "press". Fairly over the top, considering it's a school newspaper.'

'It's going to be more than a school newspaper now you're editing it,' Xanthe breathed.

'Why, thank you, Xanthe,' Chuk said with a grin.

'Anyway,' Penny said, glaring at Xanthe, 'we wanted to do a bit of digging on him.'

'OK, why?' Chuk asked.

'Well, he clearly doesn't like teaching,' Penny said.

'There are lots of teachers who don't like teaching,' Chuk said.

'But he doesn't need to do it,' Penny said. 'So, why is he here?'

'Money troubles?' Chuk shrugged. 'He's preparing for a new show. Maybe he wanted to get out of London so he could focus on it.'

'He seems to be fairly . . . unhappy,' Penny said. 'His behaviour has got a bit out of control and we were just wondering if there may be a reason for it.'

Chuk thought for a moment. 'Look,' he began, 'I'm pleased you guys are so keen, but I can't sanction you investigating a teacher. Cornwall's eccentric, true, but I think you're getting into dangerous territory here.'

'But we just wanted to keep an eye on him, see if he's up to anything unusual,' Penny said.

'I'm sorry, I just don't think it's a good idea,' Chuk said.

'But we thought you wanted to make *The Whisper* better. To stop writing about school dinners and missing library books!' Xanthe said.

141

'And I do! But we have to be careful about prying into people's lives, especially teachers,' Chuk said. 'I don't want to publish the same stuff as my father, and if Long-Pitt caught so much as a whiff of that sort of thing I'd be sacked as editor.'

'Something is definitely going on,' Xanthe said.

'Yeah, he keeps on chucking you out of his class, that's what's going on,' Chuk said.

Xanthe blushed. 'How did you –'

'Because I do my homework,' Chuk said. 'Look, I get that you don't like him. He does seem a bit . . . intense. But that's hardly unusual around here.'

'I suppose,' Penny said, not convinced.

'No need to look so glum about it!' Chuk laughed. 'If it makes you feel any better I'll keep my ears open. If I hear anything suspicious about Cornwall then you'll be the first to know. In the meantime, a new shop's opened in Grimstone, a joke shop – it looks quite cool. Go down there and interview the owner, see if we can get a discount for *The Whisper* readers.'

'Are you fobbing us off?' Penny said.

'No,' Chuk sighed, 'I'm trying to make sure you don't get expelled for writing an exposé of our most famous teacher.'

'What're you two doing here?' Arthur asked as Xanthe and Penny climbed on to the bus.

'We've got to review the new joke shop,' Penny replied.

'Lucky!' George moaned.

'I'm going to eat a lot of cake,' Arthur said smugly. 'Mrs Todd promised a Battenberg today.'

'I hate you all,' George said as he tied the laces on his football boots. 'I hope the cake is full of poison.'

The cake was delicious, and Arthur had eaten three slices before the tea was poured. He couldn't help but notice that Mrs Todd looked a little tired, her make-up was even more haphazard than usual, and her hands were shaking as she poured the tea.

'Let me do that,' Arthur said, taking the teapot from her. 'Are you all right?'

'I'm just old, Arthur,' Mrs Todd replied, leaning back in her chintz chair. 'It's dreadful being old. Never do it.'

'I'll try not to.' Arthur grinned as he sipped his tea and glanced around the room. The house looked rather shambolic. Arthur spotted the tea tray from his last visit gathering dust on the windowsill, the biscuits mouldering and the tea dregs covered in a green and lumpy fuzz.

Mrs Todd had fallen into a snooze, so Arthur quietly picked up the tray and took it into the kitchen. The sink was already filled with plates that looked as though they had been there for months. Arthur rolled up his sleeves, and got scrubbing.

There was that feeling again.

He looked out at the woods through the kitchen window. Did he see a figure step behind one of the trees? It was impossible to tell; it may have just been a branch moving in the wind, or a fox disappearing into the undergrowth.

He finished the washing-up, pushing the uneasy feelings down into the pit of his stomach.

When he walked back into the sitting room, Mrs Todd woke with a start.

'I'm so sorry, Arthur,' she said. 'I must have dozed off. You haven't been clearing up, have you?'

'It's no problem, Mrs T, it was only a few mugs, that's what I'm here for,' Arthur said. 'Are you feeling all right? Would you like me to call anyone? A doctor? One of your kids?'

'Oh, you won't want to call them,' Mrs Todd chuckled. 'You'll never get away!'

'As long as you're sure?'

'Certainly. Now how about a story? I think you deserve a reward for tackling the dreaded washing-up.'

HUSBAND AND WIFE

*I*t had just started to snow, and Imogen's mother wasn't even close to finishing her Christmas shopping. The West End was steaming with people. Everyone was elbowing each other out of the way to get the best bargains, and Imogen had started to flag a little.

Eventually Imogen's mother took pity on her, and pressed a five pound note into her hand. 'Get yourself a hot chocolate,' she said, nodding to a foggy café in a cobbled street nearby. 'I'll meet you back here in an hour.'

Imogen looked up at the sign on the corner of the street. CECIL COURT, it read. She peered down the small alley, tucked away from the busy streets of the West End and filled with shops selling antiquarian books and faded theatre posters. It looked as though it hadn't changed for centuries.

As she walked towards the café, she stopped in front of one

of the shop windows. It was crammed with tiny antique objects; enamelled pillboxes, Toby jugs, thimbles and carved ivory figurines all jostled for attention on a green velvet shelf. Imogen scanned the collection excitedly. As a little girl she'd had a doll's house, which she'd lovingly filled with miniature furniture, and ever since then she had always loved anything out of proportion – a scaled-down spoon on a necklace or a giant, plastic ice cream outside a corner shop gave her an Alice-in-Wonderland thrill. She pushed open the door and walked inside.

The owner of this Aladdin's cave of a shop looked up and smiled. With his gold-hooped earring and black goatee, he resembled a genie who had escaped from one of the tarnished silver lamps on display.

'May I help you?' he asked, setting aside the book that he had been reading.

'I'm just looking really,' Imogen said, suddenly shy.

'Well, there's plenty to look at,' the owner sighed. 'Sometimes I wonder how I fit it all in!'

Imogen glanced at the glass cases heaving with curiosities: he had a point.

By the desk was an umbrella stand that had been made from an elephant's foot. It was filled with an extraordinary collection of canes. Some had silver toppers in the shape of lizards and birds, their eyes made of glinting gems; others were twisted like barley sugars, or carved to look as though they had scales.

'My mother collected those,' the owner said, nodding at the canes. 'We have dozens more downstairs.'

Imogen carefully browsed through them. Her father shared her love of the strange, and she still hadn't found him a Christmas present.

'Are they very expensive?' Imogen asked.

The shopkeeper looked at her kindly. 'Some of them,' he admitted. 'But I'm sure I can make an exception. I don't see many collectors as young as you.'

Imogen nodded gratefully, scrutinising each stick diligently, determined to get the perfect one.

'Wow,' she said, pulling one of them out of the stand. 'This is amazing.'

The owner craned forward to look.

At first glance, the cane was not particularly exciting compared with some of the more ostentatious examples. It was made of plain, dark wood and had a simple pewter topper, but if you viewed it from above, it revealed a flat glass window. Inside were two dice, carved with peculiar symbols.

'Goodness,' the owner said. 'Do you know, I have never noticed that? You've a good eye.'

From the bowels of the shop, down a rickety staircase, a phone rang. The owner sighed.

'I shan't be a minute,' he said, hauling himself out of his leather armchair and disappearing into the basement.

Imogen looked into the cane again. One of the dice was black; the other red. Three of the sides on the black die had

147

suns carved on to them, and the other three bore moons. The red die was more varied. As Imogen delicately turned the cane, the faces revealed six different symbols: a top hat, a heart, a pair of clasped hands, a dagger, a closed eye and a dove.

Imogen marvelled at the intricacy of the design; the carvings were minuscule, but rendered in astonishing detail.

She looked around to check that the owner was still downstairs – she needn't have, as she could hear his muffled voice from below – and then gave the cane a satisfying rattle.

The rattle seemed to have a peculiar effect on the contents of the shop. The jugs and boxes and vases that crammed the shelves gave out a high, piercing whine, as though someone had run a wet finger around the rim of a wine glass.

Imogen panicked and stuffed the cane back into the stand, fleeing the shop, nervous that she might have broken something, and knowing that she would be unable to pay for it if she had.

Cecil Court, which only a moment before had been full of shoppers and pedestrians, was now empty. The windows were dimmer than they had been, and the customers in the shops were oddly still, like wax statues; a woman with her hand outstretched waiting for change, a man staring unblinking at a bookshelf.

A rolling fog began to creep down the narrow street, curling around the single lamppost and giving everything a bile-coloured tinge. Imogen could see people past the mouth of Cecil Court, hurrying along normally, but they seemed a

lifetime away. She felt as though she was a [text obscured]
behind the curved glass of a snow globe that [text obscured]
shaken, clouding up the water inside.

Suddenly Imogen heard a faint rattling, followed by footsteps. She could feel her skin prickle. A figure, tall and dashingly attired, appeared from the cloud of fog and leaned against the lamppost. He was wearing a tall top hat, and a tailcoat, and once he spied Imogen, he gave a low, sweeping bow.

When he straightened up, Imogen could see the yellow of his eyes, and the sharp, wasted features of a once-handsome face. He was carrying the cane that Imogen had so recently been examining, his bony, blue-veined hand caressing the top. He coughed, and a cloud of dust burst from his lungs.

'Please forgive me, my dear,' he said, giving Imogen a sly smile, revealing his blackened tongue and teeth. 'You woke me from a deep slumber.'

Imogen backed away from the man, trying not to look at his face.

'I'm sorry,' she said, keeping her voice as steady as she could. 'I didn't mean to wake you.'

'Then perhaps you shouldn't go poking around, eh? That's my cane you were toying with,' the man said, following Imogen as she stumbled backwards. Cecil Court suddenly seemed endless. Every time she thought she had neared the end of it, it was as though she had started back at the beginning again, as if the whole street were merely the rolling backdrop in a theatre.

'I'm very sorry, sir,' Imogen stammered. 'I didn't know. Who are you?'

'I am Husband,' he said, his black tongue snaking over his jagged teeth. 'Would you like to meet my wife?'

Before Imogen could answer, Husband whipped his top hat from his head and placed it on the ground between them.

Slowly, a skeletal hand reached out from within the hat, grasping the dusty brim. A second hand appeared, as chapped and cobwebbed as the first, and groped blindly out at the wet street, its fingers scuttling across the ground. Part by part, a creature hauled itself out of the hat, like a macabre magic trick. It was human-shaped and human-sized, but it did not move like a human. It scurried from side to side, oily, black hair obscuring its face, its torso crouched in the centre of its long trailing limbs like a spider.

'Hello, Wife,' Husband said fondly.

The creature blinked up at him, its huge black eyes just visible through the greasy hair. It hastened towards him and rubbed its head against his hand, emitting a strange clicking sound, like a beetle purring.

Husband looked at Imogen, who had turned almost as grey as his teeth with terror.

'So,' he said, 'you want to play?'

'No . . . no, thank you,' Imogen whispered.

Husband laughed. 'I'm afraid you have to play – you woke me up, you see.' He spread out his hands, as though it couldn't be helped. Wife clicked excitedly.

'Let me explain the rules,' Husband said, spinning his cane around in his hands like a baton. 'It's very simple really. You shake the dice. If the black die shows a sun, you are free to go . . . I will disappear, and all will be well.'

'And if it shows a moon?' Imogen said faintly.

Husband smiled wickedly. 'Well, if it shows a moon, then I am afraid the news is not so good.'

'What does the moon mean?' Imogen asked, sweat at her temples.

'Death,' Husband said glibly, as though he were explaining the rules to backgammon.

Imogen thought she might pass out.

'But I am nothing if not fair,' Husband said. 'It is unlikely to be you who dies.'

'Unlikely?' Imogen whispered hoarsely.

Husband nodded. 'The red die has many options. The chance of rolling your own death is a mere one in six!'

'Great,' Imogen muttered.

'Six faces, six symbols, six chances,' Husband said gaily, warming to his theme.

'The top hat,' he said, giving another swooping bow, 'is me. The heart: you. The clasped hands: a friend. The dagger: an enemy. The closed eye: a stranger. And the dove –' he paused distastefully – 'the dove means that no one is to be harmed.'

'So I'd better not roll a moon then,' Imogen murmured nervously.

151

'I knew you'd be a worthy opponent,' Husband said, his yellow eyes glinting. Wife scratched at his legs affectionately.

'And if I refuse to play?' Imogen said, with a boldness she didn't feel.

Husband's smile disappeared. 'Then I roll for you,' he sneered.

'All right,' Imogen said, desperately hoping this was all just a nightmare, that she had gone into the steamy café and nodded off.

'All you need do,' Husband said, passing her the cane ceremoniously, 'is roll the dice.'

'I don't want to,' Imogen whispered.

Suddenly, Husband was inches from her, his foul breath on her face. 'Don't toy with me,' he hissed. 'If I want you to play, you play.'

He drew back, all smiles once more. 'Continue,' he said with a greasy smile.

Imogen closed her eyes. She could hear Wife clicking and scrabbling. She shook the cane.

The dice seemed to roll for minutes, tumbling over each other, as though each were struggling for a different outcome. Every time they looked as though they might settle, they began to clatter around again.

'The battle of good and evil,' Husband said coyly. 'It always takes time.'

After a few more moments, the dice settled. Imogen dared not look down.

Wife began to screech with excitement, scuttling up the lamppost and down again.

'Come on, then, girl!' Husband said impatiently, grey spit gathering at the corners of his mouth. 'We haven't played in a long time. Wife is hungry.'

Imogen glanced down at the dice. The black die had settled on top of the red.

'What is it? What is it?' Husband demanded.

'A moon,' Imogen said hoarsely.

Husband grinned. 'And the red?' he said.

Imogen tilted the cane so that she could see the red die beneath. The relief that flooded through her was quickly replaced by a rush of bitter guilt.

'The closed eye,' she whispered.

Husband pouted. 'A stranger,' he sighed. 'Not as much fun as a friend, but beggars cannot be choosers.'

'Who will it be?' Imogen asked, her mouth dry.

Husband thought for a moment. 'Lady's choice!' he said.

'What?' Imogen asked.

'You choose!'

Husband indicated the street behind them, where the Christmas shoppers were hurrying along under their woolly hats and scarves.

'I can't!' Imogen said.

'You can, and you will,' Husband said silkily. 'Or you forfeit.'

Imogen looked at the people's faces, red from the cold and wet with sleet. She thought about their families, their homes,

153

what they might have for dinner, what they did for a living. Every time she thought she might have a candidate, an old woman muttering to herself or a man with a shaved head aggressively shouldering his way through the crowds, a thought would come into her mind: What if he has a dog? What if she has a sister who depends on her? What if he is going to write the greatest book of the century?

Husband rattled his cane threateningly. 'Tick tock,' he sang.

A girl turned the corner, talking to a friend. Imogen saw a flash of golden hair, and a white throat as the girl threw back her head and laughed. Imogen dared not look at her face.

'Her,' Imogen said, her voice flat.

Husband's eyes slid over to the girl.

Before Imogen could cry out a warning, Wife had darted out of Cecil Court and disappeared into the crowd. No one appeared to notice her; the mass of people carried on, utterly oblivious to the creature at their feet.

They seemed oblivious, too, to the girl, as Wife grabbed her by her blonde hair and dragged her screaming towards Husband. Imogen shrank into the doorway of a shop, as Wife clambered back into the hat, yanking the girl in after her.

Everything was still. Imogen thought she could hear the echo of a scream from deep, deep below the ground, but she couldn't be certain.

Husband picked his top hat up from the floor and swept it back on to his head.

154

'What a pleasure to meet you, my dear,' he said and, with a final bow, he disappeared back into the fog.

Cecil Court came back to life. Tills rang, Christmas carols resumed and the jolly owner of the antiques shop was back in his leather armchair. No one paid any attention to Imogen, leaning against the lamppost, pale and shivering, or to the stolen girl's baffled friend, who shouted her name into the cold night, wondering where she could have got to.

Arthur shut Mrs Todd's front door quietly. She had fallen asleep after finishing her story and he hadn't wanted to wake her. It meant leaving a little early, but he was sure she wouldn't mind.

It was a bitterly cold evening, and after the story of Husband and Wife the woods seemed even more hostile than before. Once again, Arthur tried not to remember the missing children and the long fingernail in the tree trunk. He kept his eyes on the path ahead, not wanting to look at the forest. It was getting dark and the birds had stopped singing. There was only the sound of the ground under his feet and the branches whispering.

A noise made Arthur look up. There was someone standing on the path ahead of him. Arthur very nearly turned to run, but then he realised who it was.

'Professor Long-Pitt!' he said. 'You nearly gave me a heart attack.'

'The brave Arthur Bannister? Surely not,' she smirked.

155

'What are you doing here?' he blurted out.

'Not that it is any of your concern,' she replied thinly, 'but I often walk in these woods in the evening. I could ask the same thing of you.'

'I've just been visiting Mrs Todd,' he said.

'You're leaving a little early, aren't you?' Long-Pitt said. 'Wednesday Afternoon Activities don't finish until five.'

'She fell asleep – I didn't want to disturb her,' Arthur said, a little tersely.

'I see. This is a perfect excuse to get on with your *Dorian Gray* essay, then.'

Arthur nodded. He had completely forgotten about that essay.

'Well, don't let me keep you,' Long-Pitt said.

Arthur stood aside awkwardly, and Long-Pitt passed him, walking into the darkness of the woods. He watched her go for a moment, puzzled, and then carried on his way to Grimstone.

CHAPTER TWELVE

Xanthe stifled a yawn. Mrs Farkin of Farkin's Joke Shop seemed to be the unlikeliest person in the world to own a shop, the sole purpose of which was to amuse. Dour, grey-haired and with a high, whining voice that would make a mosquito sound husky, Mrs Farkin had all the charisma of an egg with a face painted on it.

Xanthe and Penny had been interviewing her for half an hour, and hadn't received a single sound bite worth printing. Even though the shop itself was a cornucopia of blood capsules, masks, feather boas and magic top hats, Mrs Farkin sat in it with the stubborn grimness of a nun at a nudist colony.

'So, what's your favourite joke?' Penny asked desperately.

Mrs Farkin thought for a moment. 'I don't know any jokes,' she said finally.

Penny was just wondering whether she should make a point of stabbing herself with one of Mrs Farkin's fake swords when the doorbell tinkled and Arthur stepped in.

'Arthur!' Xanthe said, coquettishly twirling the plastic pearls she was trying on.

'Arthur,' Penny cried. 'Thank goodness! Can you think of any questions for Mrs Farkin here?'

'Er . . .' Arthur said. 'Yep. What's behind that curtain?'

He nodded at a turquoise, sequinned curtain that sealed off a section of the shop.

'Oh, that,' Mrs Farkin droned. 'That's for the cartomancer.'

'The what?' Penny asked.

'The cartomancer. He's going to read cards here once a week. Or he'll give you a crystal-ball reading. A tenner a go.'

'Could you give us a free trial?' Penny asked. 'So we could write about it in the paper?'

Mrs Farkin sighed. 'I suppose so,' she said. 'It'll give him something to do. No one's been in to see him yet.'

'It might be an idea to tell people he's in there,' Penny said.

'I didn't ask you, did I?' Mrs Farkin snapped.

She parted the curtain. 'ALAN,' she yelled. 'CUSTOMER!'

There was a loud snort, as though someone had just woken up, followed by a flurry of movement, and then a man poked his head out of the curtain. He was the colour

158

of a carrot, with an elaborate moustache that looked as though it had been very recently stuck on.

'The name is *Xanadu!*' he hissed at Mrs Farkin.

'All right, Alan. Don't get your knickers in a twist,' Mrs Farkin replied mildly.

Alan gave Mrs Farkin a look of pure hatred, and then flashed Xanthe a dazzling white smile. 'Who would like their future told?' he said in a low, warbling voice. 'Is it you, my dear?'

'No, not for me,' Xanthe said. 'Don't believe in it.'

'All right, then, what about you?' he asked Penny.

'Sure.' Penny shrugged.

'Wonderful!' Alan cried. 'Come in, child, and I will show you the wonders of the universe.'

He ushered Penny inside. Xanthe and Arthur tried to follow, but he held up his orange palm. 'I'm afraid the wonders of the universe can only be revealed one at a time,' he said, and snatched the curtain closed.

Arthur and Xanthe looked around the shop while they waited.

'So, do you like Grimstone?' Arthur asked Mrs Farkin, once the silence became too awkward.

'Not really,' Mrs Farkin yawned.

'Don't bother,' Xanthe whispered to Arthur.

After ten minutes, Penny appeared looking completely baffled.

'How did that go?' Xanthe asked hopefully.

'Absolute nonsense,' Penny whispered. 'He didn't even know the names of the cards, and I think his crystal ball is a paperweight.'

Alan whipped his sequinned cape back in a mysterious manner, and got it caught on a chair.

'I fear the young lady is too enigmatic to do an adequate reading,' he murmured, pointing at Penny. 'A great fog of mystery hangs around you, my dear!'

'A great fog of farts, more like,' Xanthe scoffed.

'What about the young gentleman? Perhaps you would like your future told, sir?'

Arthur shook his head.

'Oh, come on, Arthur. Please,' Penny begged. 'We've got to write *something* for this article.'

'OK, fine.' Arthur shrugged.

'Marvellous,' Alan said, clapping his hands, which were bedecked with colourful rings that looked as though they had come straight from Mrs Farkin's cabinet of plastic jewellery.

Alan ushered Arthur into his tiny room. It had been decorated with black, velvet drapes and a few rather un-convincing papier-mâché skulls. A small round table sat in the middle, covered with a purple satin sheet.

'What will you choose?' Alan said. 'The mystical cards? Or the glimmering crystal?'

'Um . . . the cards.' Arthur shrugged again.

'Right,' Alan said, his act slipping somewhat as he

inexpertly tried to shuffle the cards and gave himself a paper cut.

Alan laid down five cards and looked at them blankly. Arthur leaned forward.

'Right,' Alan said. 'So your first card is the River. Ever lived near a river?'

'Nope,' Arthur answered.

'Right, well, sometimes the cards are a bit vague, so the next one is . . . a skull. Oh dear. A bad omen there. Probably. Er . . . and then we have . . . a fire.'

Alan groped for a meaning for a moment.

'Ever been in a fire?' he asked hopefully.

'Should we do the crystal ball instead, Alan?' Arthur sighed.

'It is not Alan!' Alan snapped. 'It's Xanadu.'

'All right, Xanadu, shall we do the crystal ball instead? You don't seem to be having much luck with the cards.'

'Well, all right,' Alan sulked, and lifted the crystal ball on to the table.

'I have to light the candles first,' he said, putting a match to a few vanilla-scented tea lights.

'Now,' Alan said, his face illuminated by the candles, 'I shall ask the spirits to show me your fortune.' He cleared his throat and spread his arms out theatrically. 'Show me his fortune please, spirits!'

Alan looked down at his crystal ball. After a few moments, he frowned.

'What's this?' he whispered. 'How . . . ?'

Arthur leaned forward; he couldn't see a thing except the bubbles trapped in the green glass.

Alan suddenly looked up at him fearfully.

'What's going on?' Alan said. 'Is this a trick?'

'What do you mean?' Arthur asked.

'I don't like it,' Alan whimpered, staring into the ball. 'Make it stop.'

Alan was actually rather good at this, Arthur thought; he even had sweat beading on his orange forehead.

'What have you brought here?' Alan asked hoarsely, grabbing Arthur by his shoulders.

'Woah, hang on,' Arthur said, pulling away.

'Get out,' Alan squealed. 'GET OUT!'

Arthur sped out of the room and back into Mrs Farkin's shop, where Penny and Xanthe were waiting with their mouths open.

'What on earth happened in there?' Penny said.

Before Arthur could answer, Alan appeared from behind the curtain, panting, his moustache hanging from his upper lip.

'All of you get out now!' he yelled.

'Steady on, Alan,' Mrs Farkin said. 'They'll write about this in their school paper.'

'I don't care. Don't ever let them in again,' he cried.

'All right, you three,' Mrs Farkin said, 'you've upset poor Alan. Out with the lot of you.'

Arthur, Penny and Xanthe left the shop in a state of utter bewilderment.

'What on earth was that all about?' Penny asked.

'What did you do to him?' Xanthe said.

'I honestly have no idea,' Arthur replied, looking back in through the shop window.

'Well,' Penny sighed, 'at least we have a story.'

CHAPTER THIRTEEN

George was very annoyed that he had missed the excitement in Farkin's Joke Shop, especially since he had nearly had his teeth 'accidentally' knocked out by one of the Forge triplets during football.

The following morning at breakfast they were all discussing Alan's strange behaviour, when Chuk appeared over Penny's shoulder.

'Can I talk to you?' he asked.

'O-of course,' Penny stammered. She stood up awkwardly, quickly wiping jam from her cheek.

'Do you want to talk to me too?' Xanthe asked hopefully.

'No, just Penny will do, thanks,' Chuk said, as he led Penny away.

'Ouch,' George said once they were out of earshot. 'Still, you'll always have Arthur.'

'Shut up, George,' Xanthe and Arthur said in unison.

'What do you suppose they're talking about?' Jake asked, trying to hide his jealousy.

'Oh, probably just planning their wedding,' George replied.

'Shut up, George,' Jake muttered.

'What, is it "Shut Up, George" Day now?' George said.

'Every day is "Shut Up, George" Day,' Arthur answered, with a smile.

Chuk and Penny sat down on the edge of the mermaid fountain.

'Sorry to grab you like that, Penny,' Chuk said. 'But I've been thinking about what you and Xanthe said yesterday. About Cornwall.'

'Okaaay,' Penny answered.

'I did a little research last night, and you're right. Something doesn't add up.'

'What did you find?' Penny whispered.

'I spoke to one of the journalists at Dad's paper. Apparently Cornwall got into some sort of trouble in London. He disappeared in the middle of the night, obviously came here to lie low. He's in the bad books of some fairly scary people.'

'Well, judging by the conversation in the maze, they've caught up with him,' Penny reasoned. 'Poor Cornwall.'

'Hold your sympathy – we don't know what he's done yet.'

'Good point,' Penny replied. 'What do you want me to do?'

'Nothing for the time being. Just keep an eye on him, and make sure your friends do too. Let me know if you notice anything weird. I'll go to his gallery during half-term, see if anything seems suspicious.'

'No problem,' Penny said.

The bell rang for lessons.

'Right,' Penny said, hopping off the fountain. 'I'd better go.'

'Me too,' Chuk said.

Penny was just about to walk away when something occurred to her. 'If you want me to tell my friends anyway, then why did you bring me out here?' she asked.

'Maybe I just wanted to talk to you by yourself.' Chuk grinned.

By the time Penny had remembered how to talk, Chuk was already halfway to his lesson.

'I'm not sure about this,' Jake said uneasily, when Penny explained the situation to her friends at break time. 'What are we looking for exactly?'

'Just anything out of the ordinary, I guess,' Penny said with a shrug.

'But Cornwall is out of the ordinary,' Jake said. 'He's just eccentric. We can't assume he's a dangerous lunatic because he dresses like one.'

'By that logic, George would be in prison for his floral jeans alone,' Arthur said.

'My floral jeans are amazing, and I look like a god in them,' George said. 'What about your sparkly, pink trainers?'

'Touché.'

'OK,' Xanthe said, 'we have an art class this evening after CCF.'

'Ugh. It's not CCF already. I loathe CCF,' groaned Penny.

'Yeah, I think you've made that perfectly clear, Penny,' George said. 'You know, with all the whingeing and the moaning and the complaining about it every week.'

'Well, I do,' Penny said, pouting.

That afternoon, all dressed in their camouflage, the whole of the second year had to practise making rain shelters in the Shiverton woods. The Forge triplets had thrown themselves into their role of senior cadets even more than usual, and took great pleasure in screaming at their juniors until they were purple in the face.

Arthur's shelter was as hopeless as everyone else's; he had half-heartedly draped his piece of tarpaulin over some branches and was trying to camouflage it with some wet leaves. In spite of this, when Dan Forge appeared to inspect it, he smiled and patted him awkwardly on the back. 'Well done, Bannister,' he said, the praise audibly sticking in his throat. 'Very promising.'

'Seriously. What is up with Dan?' George asked, once Dan had moved on to terrorise a girl who had made a much better shelter than Arthur.

'I really have no clue,' Arthur answered, baffled.

'Is it just me, or is everyone behaving weird around here at the moment?' George said. 'I feel like we've stepped through the looking glass.'

'Yeah. And where on earth have we stepped into?' Arthur asked.

That evening's art class got off to a bad start. Cornwall was edgier than normal, his green, satin shirt was stuck to him with sweat, and he paced around the art room frantically. Every time one of the students coughed, or scraped their chair back, Cornwall jumped and looked around wildly for the source of the noise.

'He doesn't seem well,' Jake whispered to Arthur. 'What's happened to him?'

'Stop whispering!' Cornwall yelped. 'What are you whispering about?'

'Nothing, sir,' Jake replied.

'I can't have you whispering when I'm trying to think! How am I supposed to think with you . . .' Cornwall trailed off, as though he had forgotten where he was for a moment. He glanced out of the enormous windows fearfully.

'Never mind,' Cornwall muttered. 'Just get on with your self-portraits.'

The class forced their eyes back on to their canvases. George had overreached himself, once again, and was attempting an enormous oil painting of himself dressed as a medieval knight – except that it looked more like a potato draped in ferrets. Penny was using coloured ink for her self-portrait and was rather pleased with how it was going; Xanthe was using watercolours almost as incompetently as George; Arthur had stuck with something simple and was doing a rather smudgy charcoal drawing; and Jake had made a tiny etching.

Penny looked over Jake's shoulder.

'Jake! It's amazing!' she gasped.

Jake had pictured himself sitting in a chair in an empty room, looking out into a starry night through a round window.

'But it makes me feel sort of sad,' Penny admitted.

'Sad?' Jake replied. 'Why?'

'You look so lonely,' Penny said.

'I was thinking about Mum . . .' Jake replied.

Penny suddenly leaned over and gave Jake a hug. He was so surprised, and so embarrassed, that he forgot to lift his own arms and they remained dangling limply by his sides.

Cornwall looked at Penny beadily. 'No hugging!' he yelled. Penny rolled her eyes and went back to her inks.

The sound of a phone ringing pierced the quiet of the room, and Cornwall leapt to his feet.

'What is that?' he cried.

'I think it's your phone, sir,' Arthur said.

'What?' Cornwall looked bewildered. 'Oh . . . yes.'

He struggled to fish his mobile from the pocket of his tight, paisley trousers.

George giggled.

Cornwall looked at the name on the screen. 'I have to take this,' he said hoarsely. 'Carry on with your portraits.' And with that, he walked out of the classroom.

'Woah,' Arthur said. 'What was *that*? He's completely losing his marbles.'

'I'm more interested in who's on the other end of that call,' Penny said.

Emboldened by Penny's hug, Jake volunteered.

'I'll see if I can hear anything,' he said, discretely slipping out of the door.

'Be careful,' Xanthe called after him in a low voice.

Jake followed Cornwall around the art block, past the pottery room and the screen-printing studio. He had to keep his distance, and could not quite hear the content of Cornwall's frantic whispers. Cornwall stopped in the middle of the corridor, leaving Jake exposed, only a few paces behind him. Jake swerved into an old supply cupboard and hid behind one of the shelving units.

'I will not calm down!' Cornwall's voice echoed through the hall.

Jake moved closer to the door, breathing as quietly as he could.

'I've changed my mind,' Cornwall continued; he sounded close to tears. 'It's not too late!'

Jake could faintly hear the person on the other line. They sounded angry.

'You've got to get me out of this. Didn't you hear what I said? There are children here,' Cornwall hissed. 'And *he's* here.'

There was a pause. Jake leaned in further and accidentally knocked a tin of paintbrushes from a nearby shelf. They fell to the floor with a clatter. Jake froze.

'Hold on,' he heard Cornwall say. 'I'll call you back.'

Cornwall's footsteps drew nearer; Jake pressed himself into the corner of the cupboard, behind a stack of easels.

Cornwall appeared in the doorway and Jake held his breath.

'I know you're in here,' Cornwall said.

Jake stepped out of his hiding place.

'Oh! Hello, sir,' he said as blithely as he could. 'I was just fetching a scalpel: my blade broke.'

Cornwall studied him for a moment. 'Of course,' Cornwall said steadily.

Jake reached for the scalpel, and as he did so he noticed something behind the shelves. He gasped.

Cornwall gave a hollow laugh and stepped closer to Jake.

'I really wish you hadn't seen that,' Cornwall said.

'I won't tell anyone,' Jake said. 'I promise.'

'And why don't I believe you?' Cornwall sneered.

Cornwall took the key from the lock.

'Now I'm going to lock you in,' he said, with a deranged calmness that made Jake's blood run cold. 'Be a good lad and try not to make any noise.'

A few minutes later, Cornwall reappeared in the classroom. It was nearly the end of the class.

'Sir,' Penny asked, putting up her hand after a few minutes had passed, 'have you seen Jake?'

'Jake?' Cornwall asked. 'No, why?'

After the class was dismissed, Cornwall hurried back down to the storeroom. When he opened the door it was as cold as a refrigerator.

Jake was standing in the middle of the room, an uncanny smile on his face.

'Hello, sir,' Jake said.

Before Cornwall knew what was happening, he was pinned against the door, Jake's freezing hand at his throat.

'I won't tell if you won't,' Jake whispered.

It took Cornwall a moment to work out what had happened. 'Oh no . . .' he whimpered. 'What have I done?'

'Nothing, Mr Cornwall,' Jake giggled. 'Nothing at all.'

CHAPTER FOURTEEN

Toynbee looked up from his desk and was surprised to find a pallid Arthur standing over him.

'Arthur!' Toynbee said. 'What brings you to my classroom on this fine evening? Won't you sit down? Mind the shark.'

The shark wasn't easy to miss. It was an enormous great white that lay over six desks at the back of the room, its mouth open to reveal rows and rows of vicious teeth.

'I plan to hang him from the ceiling,' Toynbee said fondly.

'Where did you find him?' Arthur asked. 'Actually, never mind . . . I wanted to talk to you about Cornwall.'

'Are you going there for half-term?' Toynbee asked.

'No . . . what? I mean Mr Cornwall, Inigo Cornwall, the art teacher.'

'Oh, Inigo! Yes, of course. I know he's rather eccentric, but I like him very much, don't you?'

'That's the problem, sir,' Arthur said. 'I think, well, me and my friends think something's wrong with him.'

'Whatever do you mean?' Toynbee asked.

Arthur told him about the conversation in the maze, and Chuk's discovery, and the more urgent fact that Jake had not returned after following Cornwall in the art block.

'Jake?' Toynbee said. 'But I saw him just a moment ago in the corridor. He looked perfectly fine to me.'

'What?' Arthur asked confused. 'But –'

'Arthur,' Toynbee said, 'I think this may be the one occasion when I tell you your imagination may be running away with you.'

Arthur didn't know what to say. He nodded.

'Oh!' Toynbee said. 'That book you gave me.' He opened his desk and took out the book. 'I've read it cover to cover, and looked up every single thing in it. It seems to me that it's just an old diary of some kind. Quite an interesting historical artefact, and rather odd in places, but I don't think it's anything to worry about.'

Toynbee handed it over.

'Well,' Arthur said quietly, 'that is a relief.'

'You'll feel better after half-term, Arthur,' Toynbee said gently. 'I think you could do with a rest.'

*

Arthur chased around the Shiverton Hall corridors looking for Jake, and finally found him in the lower-school common room, staring out of a window.

'Jake!' Arthur cried. 'Where did you go? We were so worried about you.'

Jake turned to Arthur. 'Worried,' Jake repeated. He looked a little dazed.

'Are you all right, mate?' Arthur asked. 'Did something happen with Cornwall?'

Jake stared at Arthur blankly.

'Jake?' Arthur said.

'I'm all right,' Jake said, with an odd smile.

'You don't seem all right,' Arthur said.

'I'm all right,' Jake repeated.

Arthur sighed. 'OK,' he said uneasily. 'Well, it's nearly prep time. Do you want me to walk you to Pootle?'

'If you like,' Jake said hazily.

Arthur and Jake walked in almost complete silence to Pootle, Jake's boarding house. Jake walked along like a sleepwalker, as though Arthur wasn't there. Arthur wondered whether something might have happened with Jake's mother. He tended to clam up when something was wrong.

Arthur dropped Jake off at Pootle just as the bell for prep began to ring.

Arthur cursed under his breath. He would have to take the shortcut back to Garnons. He didn't like to cut through the woods, but he also didn't fancy getting detention for being late for prep.

The shortcut took him past Shiverton's sludge-green lake. During the day the lake was filled with first-time kayakers wobbling along the water, or unenthusiastic biology students fishing for ecology samples, but of course it was deserted now.

As with most places at Shiverton Hall, the lake had seen some unpleasantness. A woman had drowned there in the eighteenth century and there were rumours that her ghost loitered by the shore at night. Arthur couldn't see any sign of the poor woman tonight, though; it was only him and the still, glassy water, and the bulrushes and the moon.

And then it wasn't.

A breeze shivered through the trees and blew ripples across the surface of the lake. And Arthur had that dreadful feeling again.

He was not alone.

He looked out over the lake. There, in the centre, seemed to be something bubbling underneath the surface. And then all was still again. Arthur was about to leave when he heard the sound of splashing behind him.

Slowly, and with great reluctance, he turned around. In the middle of the lake was a still, outstretched hand, with long, grey fingers. Arthur looked at it with mounting horror, frozen to the spot. Slowly, the fingers began to move. Arthur couldn't work out what was happening at first, and once he did, he felt like he might be sick: the hand was waving at him.

Arthur wasn't an idiot: he ran.

He heard another splash of water, and then wet footsteps behind him. Arthur could smell the dank, lake water: the thing was close. Arthur sprinted as fast as he could, tripping over his own feet; he was gripped with terror that the hand was reaching out for him, that those grey fingers were just about to grasp his blazer and yank him back into the woods.

He ran until he reached the edge of the trees and saw Garnons' warm light in the distance. As he pelted for the door, he nearly knocked over Dan Forge.

'Oi!' Dan yelled, momentarily forgetting his recent cordiality.

'Sorry,' Arthur gasped. He turned, but nothing was behind him. The thing had slunk back into the darkness.

'I was just looking for you,' Dan said. 'Where have you been?'

'I was just walking back from Pootle,' Arthur said, catching his breath.

'Through the woods?' Dan said. 'You should be more careful.'

'Do you know what,' Arthur said, 'for once, you are completely right.'

*

Back in his room, after prep, Arthur shrugged off his blazer and wiped the cold sweat from his brow. He sank down on to his bed, trying to calm his frayed nerves, but it was no use.

He took the burned book from his trouser pocket and tossed it on his bedside table.

Eventually, too exhausted and full of adrenalin to pack for half-term, he got up to make himself a cup of tea. As he did, he noticed something odd.

He reached for his blazer with a shaking hand, and spread it out on his bed.

On the grey wool on the back of it were four long, thin tears. He tried to tell himself that they had been caused by a tree branch, desperate to rationalise it. But, it was of no use: he knew what they were.

They were scratches.

CHAPTER FIFTEEN

'I saved you a seat, Arthur,' Xanthe lisped from the back of the London bus.

As Arthur made his way down the aisle, he noticed Chuk, who waved as he walked past.

'Everything OK?' Xanthe asked as Arthur took his seat. 'You look a bit peaky.'

'Thanks,' Arthur muttered. He hadn't got much sleep the night before.

'Well, at least we have a week off now,' Xanthe said. 'Do you want to come to the cinema with me? There's a French film about mime that I want to watch.'

'Sorry, Xanthe, I'd probably better hang out at home. I haven't seen Mum and Rob for ages. Plus that film sounds terrible.'

'It's won lots of awards,' Xanthe said sniffily.

The bus rumbled along to London, the students getting louder and rowdier as they approached the city. Xanthe was busy annotating her copy of *The Picture of Dorian Gray* while Arthur looked out of his window, trying to shake off the dread that seemed to have become a constant presence in his life.

He had never been more relieved to see his mother, or his little brother Rob, who seemed to have grown a couple of inches since Arthur had last seen him. When the bus pulled into the station, he grabbed his bag, jumped off and folded them both into an enormous hug.

'Ugh!' Rob complained, wriggling out of Arthur's arms. 'Get off me!'

Halfway through the week, the novelty of being at home had worn off somewhat. Rob spent the entire time annoying him, his mother had got tired of their bickering and he missed his friends. He'd tried to call Jake, but it was impossible to get through to their landline and Jake wasn't picking up his mobile. George and Penny were miles away with no reception. By Thursday night, Arthur gave in, called Xanthe and agreed to go and see the film with her.

He arrived at the cinema in Leicester Square to find Xanthe wearing a floor-length pink dress, her hair in a stiff, beauty-queen beehive.

'You're a bit dressed up for the cinema, aren't you?' Arthur laughed.

Xanthe's whole person, including her hair, seemed to deflate.

'Sorry, I mean, you look lovely,' Arthur said quickly.

Xanthe beamed. 'Oh, this old thing!' she said, smoothing down the brand new dress. 'I wear it all the time.'

'Cool,' Arthur said, 'shall we go in?'

Once they had stocked up on popcorn, lemonade and sweets in the foyer, they made their way into the cinema. It was completely empty.

'This looks promising,' Arthur sighed.

'I know!' Xanthe replied. 'I've no idea why everyone is going to see that dinosaurs thing next door.'

'*Dinosaurs on Mars!*' Arthur cried. 'I didn't know that was on yet!'

He grumbled as they found their seats and prepared himself for an excruciating couple of hours.

About an hour into the movie, Arthur still had absolutely no idea what was going on. It was black and white, with almost no dialogue, and seemed to be about a man who had lost his cat. Xanthe sat next to him, completely absorbed.

With a sudden sinking in his stomach, Arthur had the feeling again: he was being watched.

He turned around, letting his eyes adjust to the dark. The cinema seemed empty at first glance, but then Arthur saw it. Someone sitting in the back row, close to the door.

'You're missing the film,' Xanthe whispered, elbowing him.

'Shhhh!' Arthur whispered back. 'There's someone in here with us.'

'Well, duh,' Xanthe said, 'it is a cinema.'

'No, Xanthe,' Arthur said. 'Look!'

He turned around again and pointed to the back of the cinema . . . only now it was empty.

'There's no one there, Arthur,' Xanthe said.

'But –'

'Look, if you're not enjoying the film then we can leave. You don't need to make excuses.'

'I'm not making excuses!'

Arthur got up and went to look at the back row, searching underneath the chairs. Nothing.

He settled back into his seat, his mind churning over the possibilities.

'There are only two hours left,' Xanthe said, with a comforting pat on his hand.

'*Mon chat!*' the actor cried. '*Où est mon chat?*'

Arthur wondered fleetingly whether it would have been better to have been attacked by the thing in the back of the cinema.

Arthur and Xanthe discussed the movie over an ice cream afterwards. Xanthe said it was the most moving film she had ever watched, and Arthur said that he would rather be kicked to death by a gang of mimes than ever watch it again.

They walked to the Tube together, Xanthe holding her dress out of the grimy puddles and Arthur wondering whether he was even less safe in London than he had been in Shiverton. He felt apprehensive in the crowds; it was too easy for someone to hide in them.

He walked Xanthe to the Northern Line and waited for the Tube with her. Just before the train doors opened, Xanthe quickly turned around and gave Arthur a peck on the cheek. She jumped on to the train, her face now as pink as her dress, and waved shyly as the train pulled out of the station.

Arthur wondered whether he had accidentally taken Xanthe on a date, and felt a little guilty that he hadn't cottoned on to it sooner.

He walked through Leicester Square Tube station towards the Piccadilly Line, avoiding the shouting drunks and gangs of squealing girls, and jumped on to his train as the doors were closing.

The carriage was full of people dressed up as though it was Halloween. There were sailors, bumblebees, mermaids, scarecrows, a hangman, a butterfly and someone who had dressed as Death, with a hooded, black cape and a plastic scythe.

'What's going on?' Arthur asked the man standing next to him, who was dressed as a giant prawn.

'Birthday bash in Hammersmith,' the prawn replied. 'It's a costume party. Want to come along?'

'I'm all right, thanks,' Arthur replied.

'Suit yourself,' the prawn said haughtily.

More and more revellers joined the carriage at each stop, until it was crammed with people singing and laughing. Arthur was glad of the company, even if it did mean that he could barely move, but when they all got off at Hammersmith, Arthur had had enough of out-of-tune renditions of 'Happy Birthday', so he peeled away from the crowd and headed for the lift.

As he walked down the empty tunnel, he heard the echo of footsteps behind him. He reached the lift and pressed the button frantically.

Maybe it was just another reveller in a costume. Maybe it was just a coincidence that someone had decided to dress as a hangman.

He knew he was wrong the moment he felt the hand on his arm.

'There are CCTV cameras here,' Arthur said, as the burned man pulled him to a halt.

'You don't give me much credit, do you?' the man snarled with his blunted tongue. 'The ones here are dummies.' He pointed a hairy finger at the fake camera.

Arthur tried to stay calm. Someone was bound to come around the corner any minute now.

'No one gets the lift at this time of night,' the man said

with a hoarse laugh, reading Arthur's mind. 'A bit too creepy.'

'What do you want?' Arthur asked.

'You know what I want,' the man growled. 'And I do not enjoy repeating myself. I am offering you one more chance. Do not go back to Shiverton Hall.'

'I'll take my chances there if you're here, thanks very much,' Arthur snapped back.

The man grunted. Arthur could see his eyes through their slits; warped, pink eyelids, the eyelashes singed off.

'You'll pay for your arrogance, you know,' the man said.

The man took a heavy step towards Arthur and grabbed him by both arms.

'You may think you've seen the worst of it,' he continued, 'but a few ghosties and ghoulies are the least of your worries. That place does something extra special to a boy like you.'

'What do you mean, "a boy like me"?' Arthur asked.

'A boy who already has a darkness in his blood,' the man leaned in and whispered. 'A boy called Arthur Shiverton.'

The man released Arthur from his grip and gave a sarcastic bow.

'Wait . . .' Arthur said faintly. 'How did you know?'

But the man was already walking away.

'Wait!' Arthur repeated, chasing after him. But when Arthur turned the corner the man was gone.

Chapter Sixteen

Chuk checked the slip of paper again. *66 Saturn Court*, it read. But he was standing on Saturn Court and couldn't see a number sixty-six anywhere. A girl walked out of one of the nearby galleries wearing headphones and Chuk waved for her attention.

'Yes?' she said, annoyed.

'Sorry, I'm looking for the Strack Gallery, number sixty-six,' Chuck replied.

The girl rolled her eyes. 'Oh yeah, it's so trendy that they make it impossible to find.'

She walked him over to a brick wall and pointed at a tiny, ornate doorbell in the middle of it. 'There you go,' she said.

Chuk rang the doorbell and waited. After about five minutes, a door-shaped seam appeared in the brick wall with a click. Chuk pressed it, and it slid to one side, revealing a cavernous gallery.

Chuk went inside. On the stark, white walls hung a series of enormous canvases painted black, each with a single red spatter in the middle.

'May I help you?'

Chuk turned to find himself being scornfully appraised by a woman with a shaved head and plastic glasses decorated with ants.

'Yes,' Chuk said with his most charming smile. 'Do you have anything by Inigo Cornwall?'

The woman smirked. 'I'm afraid Inigo Cornwall's work is reserved for our clients.'

Chuk smirked back. 'Then I'll tell my father, Harrison Pike, that you don't have anything for him.'

The woman panicked. 'Ha-harrison Pike?' she stammered. 'Of course. We have many things that I'm sure he'd like. Please come this way.'

He followed as her heels clattered across the glittering floor. 'Petronella!' she screamed at the pretty blonde girl sitting behind the desk. 'Get Ms Strack!'

Helena Strack appeared a few moments later, and smiled icily at her shaven-headed employee, who scuttled away in terror.

Ms Strack put out a cold hand, and Chuk shook it. She had an unsettling, alien beauty; she wore only white, which matched her snow-white hair and skin, but her long nails and her lips were painted black. Chuk wondered how old she was; she might have been anything from thirty to sixty.

'Mr Pike,' she said, in a deep voice every bit as strange as her appearance. 'You are here to see our Cornwalls?'

'For my father, yes,' Chuk replied.

'For your father, yes,' Ms Strack repeated with a faint smile. 'This way.'

'How long have you represented Mr Cornwall?' Chuk asked as Ms Strack floated through the gallery.

'Many years,' she answered. 'We're great friends.'

'Is he here?' Chuk asked. 'I'd love to meet him.'

'I'm afraid not,' she replied.

She ushered him through an antechamber filled with glass bubbles.

'This work is sold, I'm afraid,' she said.

Finally they reached the back of the gallery, a large room painted a slick black.

The room contained several large sculptures of decaying meat carved out of pink marble. Flies made of emeralds and sapphires feasted on the flesh.

'This is . . . interesting,' Chuk said, looking at the sculptures dubiously.

Strack turned on her pointed heel and looked at Chuk coolly.

'Why are you here, Mr Pike?' she asked.

'What do you mean?' Chuk asked innocently.

'Well, I know that as your father only collects Pre-Raphaelite art, he would be about as interested in these sculptures as you clearly are.'

Chuk tried to think of a response.

'I also know,' Strack continued, 'that you must already be acquainted with Inigo Cornwall, seeing that he is a teacher at your school. So let me ask you again, why are you here?'

'He's just such a great artist!' Chuk gushed with scholarly enthusiasm. 'I wanted to find out more about him, that's all.'

Strack studied Chuk's earnest face for a moment.

'Indeed,' she said softly. 'I am glad. I was worried for a moment that you had come here to pry. Which wouldn't have been a very clever idea at all, no matter who your father is.'

Chuk dropped his act.

'Is that a threat?' he asked.

'A threat?' Strack said, her pale eyes emotionless. 'I don't know what you mean.'

'Thanks for the tour, Ms Strack,' he said coolly. 'It's been extremely . . . illuminating.'

Strack gave him a terrifying smile.

'My pleasure.'

CHAPTER SEVENTEEN

Arthur boarded the bus that would take him back to Shiverton Hall. He had spent the car ride to the station constantly checking the road behind him, terrified the burned man might be following them. 'Everything all right, petal?' his mum had asked. 'Fine,' Arthur had replied, his mouth dry.

Xanthe was already sitting with someone else, although she tried to push them off the seat once she saw Arthur coming. Arthur quickly ducked into the seat next to Chuk. They discussed Strack and Cornwall all the way back to school, but by the time they pulled up to the crumbling Shiverton gates, they were still no closer to the truth.

When Arthur arrived at his room he found George lying on his bed, reading a book and eating a biscuit.

'Please! Make yourself at home!' Arthur said, brushing away the crumbs that had tumbled on to his duvet.

'Thanks, mate,' George said, oblivious to Arthur's sarcasm.

'So, how was your week?' Arthur asked.

'Brilliant, thanks,' George replied. 'I saw Grandpa.'

'Why do I feel a story coming on?' Arthur sighed.

'Because you know me too well.' George grinned. 'He told me a new story, about Lord Shiverton.'

Arthur flushed at the name. He wasn't sure he wanted to know anything more about his bloodthirsty ancestor.

'It isn't even in the book,' George sang tantalisingly.

'Why not?'

'Because he's only just found out about it. He bought a box of old Grimstone books for his archive and found an eyewitness account of the night that Rose Watkins went missing.'

'Rose Watkins?' Arthur repeated. 'You mean the witch's daughter?'

It had been the first story George had told Arthur. The story of the Shiverton Curse.

After building the hall, the ageing Lord Shiverton had become increasingly insane and depraved, and had abducted and murdered four young women from Grimstone. He did not realise that his final victim was the daughter of Ma Watkins, a powerful witch, who wreaked a fatal revenge on Lord Shiverton and put a curse on his ancestors.

'Poor Rose,' George said, 'Lord Shiverton was not the kind of man you'd want to bump into in the middle of the night.'

GRIMSTONE, 1799

'*I*'*ll be all right.*'

It was late already, and Rose Watkins didn't have time to wait for the landlady's son to finish up moving the ale barrels and chaperone her home.

'Ma will be waiting for me. I only have to walk over a field, Mrs Cratch. I do it every night, don't I?'

Rose could see that Mrs Cratch was concerned; she was twisting her pink hands around an old dishcloth, looking back into the emptying pub to see what progress her son was making.

'Please, Rosie,' Mrs Cratch begged. 'He'll only be a minute with them barrels, and I can't let a barmaid o' mine walk around by herself at night – not with all this nasty business going on. Three girls have gone missing, Rose. Don't you be the fourth.'

Rose rolled up the cotton sleeve of her dress and flexed a

muscle. 'Look at that, Mrs Cratch. Ain't going to come to no harm with these arms.' She picked up her skirts and started towards the field. 'G'night. Thanks for the pie!'

Mrs Cratch shook her head. 'Rosie Watkins! You shouldn't be cuttin' through Bradby's cornfield anyhow,' she called after Rose. 'You'll spoil the corn an' we'll all be in trouble.'

But Rose was already skipping through the field and into the night, her golden hair tied prettily with a pink ribbon shimmering behind her.

The light from the pub did not stretch far, and soon Rose was walking in the dark, with only the sound of the whispering corn and a thin crust of moon to keep her company. But Rose was as brave as any boy in the village, braver sometimes, and could find her way home with her eyes closed.

Bradby's cornfield reached over a small hill, with the Grimstone Tavern on one side and Rose's mother's cottage on the other. At the crest of the hill the view stretched for miles on every side: the lights of Grimstone, the thatch of Ma Watkins's little house, and further too . . . in the distance, dark and alone, the malevolent shadow of Shiverton Hall. Rose shuddered to look at it. She'd heard the village rumours: that it was Lord Shiverton himself who had snatched those girls.

Rose made her way up the hill, her breath catching slightly. It had been a hard day of rowdy customers and she longed for her bed.

She stopped.

Across the field, a little way away, stood a shadow.

'Who goes there?' Rose called out, her voice shaking.

The figure did not respond. Rose remained still, willing her eyes to adjust to the darkness so that she might see better. It was tall, a man – she would stake her life on it – though it had the long hair of a woman, straggled and wispy and blowing in the wind. Straight as a whip, it stood motionless amid the corn, with its arms flung out to the sides, as though crucified.

Rosie gasped, and then burst out laughing.

The scarecrow.

Of course, she thought, resuming her walk and giggling to herself. It was Farmer Bradby's scarecrow. It had frightened the wits out of her when she was a child, but in recent years she had begun to see its annual appearance as a pleasant sign that summer was on its way. She looked back at its ragged silhouette and rolled her eyes at her own girlishness. She was glad Mrs Cratch's son hadn't accompanied her tonight: he would have teased her mercilessly had he caught her trembling over an old bag of straw.

Rose stopped at the peak of the hill, as she always did on a clear night, to admire the view. The black hulk of Shiverton Hall seemed even more menacing than usual, its jagged stones exaggerated in the moonlight. Rosie pulled her shawl closer to her.

She was about to continue on when something made her pause. A rustling, faint in the wind, and the sound of footsteps in the corn behind her.

Rosie turned sharply. The scarecrow was gone.

She dropped her basket with a thud, spilling Mrs Cratch's leftover pie all over the field. She didn't care; she ran, her legs tumbling, her heart in her throat and the corn stinging her shins.

Whatever it was ran behind her, close, but she dared not turn to find out how close. She could hear it breathing, a rattling and low hiss.

Rose could see the cottage clearly now, her home, and her old mother sitting by the fire through the window. She gulped in some air to cry out when she felt the fingers snatch at her dress, pulling her back into the darkness.

Before she could scream, a cold, wet hand closed over her mouth.

The last thing Rose saw as the hunched, foul-smelling figure dragged her into the woods was Farmer Bradby's innocent scarecrow, further down the field, a silly hat on its head and a crooked red smile painted on its face.

'So it was Lord Shiverton in the field?' Arthur said with a shudder.

'The town had always wondered how Rose and the other girls went missing without anyone noticing anything. It seems Lord Shiverton stood in the field, waiting, dressed as a scarecrow and snatched them as they went by. Who would think to be suspicious of a scarecrow?'

'Who saw it happen?' Arthur asked.

'A little beggar boy,' George replied. 'He'd followed Rose secretly, hoping that he might snatch the leftover pie.'

'Why didn't he do anything? Scream?'

'Too frightened, I suppose,' George said. 'He told the vicar the following day, who transcribed his account, but it seems that he was on Lord Shiverton's payroll because the transcription was hidden and no one was told about it.'

'Ugh,' Arthur shivered. 'Imagine being chased by a scarecrow.'

'Pretty grim,' George agreed.

'Why can't we just go to a normal school?' Arthur sighed.

'Because,' George replied, 'normal is boring.'

Once George had left, Arthur settled into bed, and finally picked up the burned book. He read the ominous warning in the front, and skipped through the pages. Toynbee was right: it didn't appear to make much sense. It seemed to be a fairy story about a faceless beast, but it was so rambling and strange that Arthur could make neither head nor tail of it. When he reached the middle, he noticed that a couple of the pages had been ripped out; it looked as though the missing pages had been illustrated, as some gold ink remained on the tears at the seam.

Arthur held the book up to the light. He hoped that

the writer might have pressed a little too hard with his pen, and that some of the contents of the missing pages might have embossed themselves on the pages beneath. Sure enough, he could just about see an imprint of some letters. He walked over to his desk and took out some tracing paper and a pencil from his art folder. It was a trick he had learned in primary school, when they had made brass rubbings. He placed the tracing paper over the pages, and, holding his pencil at an angle, scribbled over the top. Gradually, a word emerged:

SCRACCHENSHODDEREN

CHAPTER EIGHTEEN

'Did you hear about Jake?' Penny asked Arthur and George as they settled in next to her in the art block.

'No,' Arthur said. 'Is everything all right?'

'He's staying at home for the rest of term,' Penny whispered. 'His mum wrote a letter to the school.'

'I wonder what's up,' George said. 'Don't you think he was acting a bit weird before we left for half-term?'

'Tell me about it,' Arthur said. 'He was like a zombie.'

Cornwall crashed into the classroom. He looked dreadful. Clothes that had been tight when he first arrived now hung off him, and he had deep purple rings around his eyes.

'Are you all right, sir?' George asked, as Cornwall crashed into an easel.

'Do I look all right?' Cornwall hissed. The class looked up at him in surprise.

Cornwall shook himself out of it, forcing a laugh. 'Of course I'm all right,' he said, ruffling George's hair awkwardly. 'Never been better.'

The term crept by with all the slowness of a star imploding. The only thing Arthur looked forward to were his visits to Mrs Todd, who always cheered him up with her unspeakably horrible stories. It surprised him that he enjoyed these dark tales so much, given his own past, and wondered whether George's love of the macabre had finally rubbed off on him.

Penny, Xanthe and Chuk had no luck in discovering any more about Cornwall, in spite of their diligent research.

'He seems to have just appeared from nowhere,' Chuk had said frustratedly one Wednesday afternoon. 'He had his first show in 1999, but before that . . . nothing.'

All the time, Arthur had the sense that he was being followed. It had become so frequent that he was almost used to the sensation.

He had gone to the library one evening to pick out some books about Oscar Wilde. He'd got a B- from Long-Pitt for his last *Dorian Gray* essay, and was determined to do better on the next one. The library was empty, except for Miss Hartley, one of the school librarians. Arthur looked up at the Gainsborough hanging over the fireplace, the Creeper lurking as malevolently as ever in the distance.

He passed his books to Miss Hartley, who smiled up at him. He liked Miss Hartley, who was always kind to everyone, and almost never fined students for handing books in late. She had been blinded in a riding accident a few years before, and it always struck Arthur as something of a tragedy that she could no longer read the books that she checked in and out of the library, although she listened to audio books when the library wasn't busy. One of her earphones was still in her ear as she processed Arthur's books.

'What are you listening to?' Arthur asked.

'*Wuthering Heights*,' Miss Hartley said. 'It's one of my favourites. I think Long-Pitt is teaching it next term.'

'Is it long?' Arthur asked.

'Not very,' Miss Hartley laughed. 'And it's very good.'

She scanned the last book through and passed it back to Arthur.

'Right,' she said. 'You have these for a week. Enjoy!'

'Thanks,' he said.

'You're welcome. Now, what would your friend like to check out?'

Arthur paused.

'I'm sorry, Miss Hartley, but it's just me here.'

'Don't tease me,' Miss Hartley said. 'There's another boy in here. I know it.'

Arthur looked around him: it was just him and Miss Hartley in the room.

201

'He's standing next to you,' Miss Hartley added.

Arthur felt his stomach squirm.

'I promise you,' he said slowly, 'there isn't anyone here.'

Miss Hartley cocked her head. 'How very strange. I could have sworn . . .' She listened for a moment.

'Never mind,' she sighed. 'I must be imagining things. Have a nice evening, Arthur.'

'You too,' Arthur said hoarsely.

The walk to Mrs Todd's house the following Wednesday was unbearable. Since the conversation with Miss Hartley, Arthur had felt increasingly haunted. He had barely slept, convinced he could see shadows moving out of the corners, and the prospect of entering the woods, with all their dark hiding places, made him turn white with icy terror. He had asked George to come with him, but he had been unable to get out of his own WAA, and so Arthur was forced to walk through the woods alone.

The relief he felt when he saw Mrs Todd open the door was overwhelming.

'Come in, Arthur,' she said. 'Are you all right? You look dreadful.'

'I'm all right,' he replied. 'I've not been sleeping very well, that's all.'

'At Shiverton Hall?' she said. 'I'm not surprised. I wouldn't want to sleep there either.'

Arthur smiled weakly as she poured him a cup of tea.

'I was thinking about that place again yesterday,' Mrs Todd said bitterly. 'They should never have turned it into a school.'

'It wasn't the best plan in the world,' Arthur agreed grimly.

'Long-Pitt, in all her arrogance, thinks she can keep the place safe,' Mrs Todd said. 'Madness. Particularly after what happened when she became headmistress. You would have thought that might have taught her a lesson!'

'What do you mean?' Arthur asked.

'The terrible accident – you must have heard of it. But, then, I suppose it was before your time.'

'I know I'm probably going to regret asking this,' Arthur said, 'but what happened?'

THE GRIMSTONE WITCHES

*T*here have always been witches in Grimstone. Or, at least, that is what the people of Grimstone have always believed. The village burned more women than any other place in England, according to the records, and the ones that they didn't burn they drowned in the river. Most of these women were innocent, accused of witchcraft because they practised homeopathy or because a certain crop had failed that year; often the accusations had no basis whatsoever and simply provided a way for a husband to rid himself of a wife he no longer wanted. But there was one case where even the sceptics had no quibble about the verdict.

The girl was called Ann and she was about ten years old, although no one could be sure of that. She had no last name, for she had no family. One morning she had simply appeared in the village, begging for scraps. She had a cherubic appearance, with curled blonde hair and black eyes that glittered like opals, and for that reason she was soon taken in by the miller and his family, who treated her as one of their own. The Millers already had three children: strapping, healthy boys, who had grown tall and strong on the miller's bread. But Mrs Miller had always pined for a girl, and it seemed that Ann was the perfect child to fulfil the role. Ann was beautiful, polite and well spoken – surprisingly so for a beggar child. Mrs Miller believed that Ann was a high-born child who had been orphaned, although when pressed, Ann would not verify this. In fact, she would not speak of her past at all.

It was not long after Ann first arrived that the Millers' eldest child caught a fever. The boy was covered in a rash of purple spots and was tormented by terrible hallucinations, but the physician could not identify the illness, telling the boy's terrified parents that the only option was to wait.

After a week of the boy's night terrors, which seemed to be building in frequency and volume, Ann shyly approached Mrs Miller. She said that her grandmother had been an apothecary and had taught her the healing properties of plants. If Mrs Miller so wished, Ann could concoct a tonic that might soothe her son. Mrs Miller and her husband were desperate and quickly agreed for Ann to retrieve the relevant plants from the woods.

Ann returned to the house with handfuls of flowers and weeds, and began work in the Millers' kitchen, muttering under her breath as she did so.

She made an elixir for the elder Master Miller, and a different one for the younger boys, in order to prevent them from catching the sickness themselves.

The following day the boy's fever had subsided, and the day after that the rash disappeared. The Millers were overjoyed, and soon word spread of Ann's healing potions. It was not long before every parent in Grimstone was queueing up at the Millers' door to buy Ann's tonic for their children. It was to be taken weekly, Ann instructed them, in order to keep them healthy and immune to disease.

After a few weeks, it became clear that the tonic wasn't working. The children of Grimstone began to sicken, all of them with the same symptoms. They seemed lethargic, their eyes were glazed and their skin had taken on a greenish hue. Parents turned up at the Millers' demanding more potions from Ann, but it seemed the more they fed the potions to their children, the sicker they got.

Three children died of this mystery illness, until the physician began to wonder whether Ann's potion was the cause of the sickness itself. He immediately ordered that all the children stop taking it. Their health gradually improved, and it was then that the physician made the first accusation of witchcraft. Soon, other fingers pointed in Ann's direction too, and the Millers cast her out of their house.

Ann was ruled a poisoner and a witch, and sentenced to death by burning.

On the day of the burning, the town gathered around the pyre, the parents of the dead children screaming abuse at young Ann as she calmly allowed herself to be tied to the stake. As the fires were lit, a black storm gathered in the sky above her head, and a deluge of rain not seen for a hundred years struck the town. The kindling beneath Ann's dainty feet fizzled and died.

This was taken as further proof of Ann's guilt and she was dragged to the river, the crowd baying behind her. They tied her to a heavy wooden chair and threw her into the deepest part to much cheering.

The following morning the town watched as she was hauled out of the water, dripping wet, her head slumped. The chair was placed on the shingle by the river: no one dared approach it.

Ann's head moved, and the crowd gasped. Slowly, she looked up, water running down her face, and laughed.

The village did not know what to do. Every other witch they had put to death had actually died. A few of the men stayed up in the church that night, guarding Ann, trying to ignore her as she sat giggling in the corner, and debating what they should do with her.

There was a well in the woods past the hills, one of the men said, that had dried up a few decades before. He suggested that Ann be thrown into it, and the mouth of the well sealed up. It was decided, and the following day, at the break of dawn, Ann was thrown into the well. She did not struggle or even scream, but muttered under her breath, her skin so burning hot that the men had to wear leather gloves to hold her.

The well was hammered shut with wooden planks and the strongest nails the blacksmith could forge. As the last plank was laid down, the men swore they could hear singing, echoing up from the well's depths, but as the final nail was hammered in, the sound was sealed inside.

Hundreds of years later, after Shiverton Hall had been built and turned in a school, the new headmistress, Professor Long-Pitt, was walking through the woods when she came across the well. The planks had all but rotted to dust and she pulled the remaining shards away. She had grown up at the hall – her father had been headmaster – and had walked the woods countless times as a girl, but she had never noticed the well.

Her plans for the school included building a kitchen garden, one that the students could tend themselves, and she realised that this clearing would be an ideal spot. The children could use the water from the well whenever the plants needed watering.

During the summer holidays the gardener set to work, and by the time term started, the kitchen garden was ready for the students, who took to it enthusiastically.

It was unfortunate, therefore, that after a few weeks, one of the students who had been in charge of the garden fell ill. Her hands were raw and blistered. The doctor thought at first that she might be allergic to one of the plants, but as the boils began to spread up her arms and around her throat, this *seemed increasingly unlikely. After two further students who had been working on the garden started to show symptoms, Long-Pitt closed it up.*

The children's health deteriorated, and they were admitted to hospital. Long-Pitt had the soil tested, but found nothing. It was only when a doctor examined the children for toxins that they discovered what had happened: someone had been poisoning the water supply. Two of the children were saved by this discovery, but it was too late for the youngest, a girl in the first year, who died.

When the well was dredged, they found the ancient skeleton of a girl inside, but how the water had been poisoned remained a mystery.

It was only Long-Pitt who had her suspicions. There had always been witches near Grimstone, after all.

'I've never heard that story before,' Arthur said.

'And you won't hear it,' Mrs Todd said. 'Long-Pitt has a knack for covering these things up. You have to be very good at keeping secrets at Shiverton Hall.'

Arthur thought about his own secrets.

'I've never really been Long-Pitt's biggest fan,' he said.

'Wise,' Mrs Todd said quietly.

'What was that?' Arthur asked.

'Oh, nothing,' Mrs Todd said. 'I'm just talking nonsense in my old age. Why don't you take off early, Arthur? You don't want to walk through those woods after dark.'

Arthur smiled gratefully and got up. 'Thanks, Mrs Todd,' he said.

'See you next week,' she replied.

'I've got to do my CCF camping trip next week,' Arthur said. 'Sorry, I forgot to say.'

'Camping?' Mrs Todd asked. 'How ghastly! Well, I hope to see you before term finishes at least.'

'Of course,' Arthur said.

As he was leaving, Mrs Todd touched his arm.

'Arthur,' she said. 'Be careful.'

Arthur nodded, and left.

Long-Pitt was standing on the path when Arthur turned out of Rose Cottage.

'Hello again, Arthur,' she said.

'Hello, Professor,' Arthur answered.

He walked past her uneasily, conscious that her eyes were on him. Once he had walked a few steps down the path, he heard her turn away and continue her walk into the woods.

'Creepy,' Arthur muttered under his breath, and tried not to think about the skeleton at the bottom of the well, or why it was that Long-Pitt seemed to be waiting for him in the woods again.

CHAPTER NINETEEN

Arthur was an hour early for the school bus. There was a regular bus that went past the Shiverton school gates, which left in ten minutes, so Arthur decided to take that one – he'd have plenty of time to walk from the gates to the hall.

As he waited at the bus stop, he spotted someone he knew across the road.

'Alan!' Arthur called. Alan looked up; he was wearing his glittery cape and had added a jewelled turban to complete the outfit. Once Alan saw Arthur, he started to run.

'Alan!' Arthur yelled. 'Wait!'

Arthur ran after him. Luckily Alan was terribly unfit, and after a few minutes he was doubled over and gasping for breath, cape spooled on the ground.

'I just wanted to talk to you!' Arthur said.

'Get away from me,' Alan replied.

'What is going on?' Arthur asked.

'You tell me!' Alan choked.

'What do you mean?'

'Listen, you,' Alan said, standing up and prodding Arthur with his finger. 'I'm not a bloody soothsayer, all right? I'm Mrs Farkin's nephew. I don't know anything about that stuff.'

'Well, that was fairly obvious,' Arthur admitted.

Alan glared at Arthur. 'She just pays me to sit in that room and spout a load of rubbish. I bought that crystal ball from a car boot sale in Reading,' Alan continued.

'It looks like a paperweight,' Arthur said.

'It is a blasted paperweight!' Alan yelled.

'OK. So why did you freak out when you read my fortune, then?' Arthur asked. 'Is that part of the act?'

'No,' Alan hissed. He looked up and down the road to check that no one was coming.

'When I looked into the glass ball, I saw something,' Alan said.

'What did you see?' Arthur asked.

Alan shook his head.

'What did you see?' Arthur repeated.

'I saw something that couldn't possibly be,' Alan said.

'What?'

'You, a reflection, I mean . . . only there was someone standing behind you.'

'Behind me?'

'At first I thought it was a trick of the light, that you had been reflected in the glass twice. But it wasn't you. There was a dark figure standing behind you, and its hands were around your neck.'

'What did it look like?' Arthur asked, feeling sick.

'I couldn't see the face,' Alan replied.

Arthur squeezed his eyes shut. The pavement slabs were shifting like water beneath his feet.

'Are you all right?' Alan asked.

'I'm fine,' Arthur said hoarsely. 'I need to catch my bus, so . . .'

Arthur staggered away, his legs weak.

'There was something else,' Alan called after him.

Arthur reluctantly turned back.

'It was later,' Alan said, 'when I was putting the cards away.'

'Go on,' Arthur said.

'I'd pulled out some cards for you before, you remember, but I couldn't read them. I've never been able to read the cards, just make it up.'

'So?' Arthur asked.

'As I was putting them away, I suddenly saw them. Really *saw* them. It was like an optical illusion, when your eyes adjust and suddenly you can see the pattern clearly.'

'And what did my cards say?' Arthur said, reluctantly.

Alan looked at his bejewelled hands uncertainly.

'Please tell me,' Arthur said. 'I'd like to know.'

'Something terrible,' Alan replied.

'Something terrible happens to me?'

'Yes . . . no . . .' Alan said uneasily. 'It's not quite that . . . although that is part of it.'

'What is it, then?'

Alan looked Arthur directly in the eye. 'You are going to do something terrible,' Alan whispered.

Arthur was the only person on the bus. He was pathetically grateful to be alone, as he felt that at any moment he might burst into tears. He couldn't tell his friends about this, not even George. They did not know about his Shiverton blood, or the burned man, or the book. It was yet another secret that Arthur would have to keep close.

Ever since that day by the reservoir, when he had attacked his tormentors and nearly killed them, Arthur had worried that he was capable of something terrible. It seemed that even Alan, a self-confessed fraud, could see the same thing. It was only a matter of time until others began to fear it too.

The bus stopped in one of the overgrown, country lanes, and a tall, thin boy in a hood loped on and sat down in the front of the bus, side-on to Arthur, who was sitting towards the back.

The fluorescent lights hummed above him, and the bus rumbled on.

Arthur didn't know whether he was being oversensitive after his conversation with Alan, but the presence of the hooded boy made him uneasy. Arthur could not see his face, his tall body hunched forward and his black hood pulled down. Arthur tried not to look: he would be at the Shiverton gates in a couple of stops. The bus driver was with them; they weren't alone.

But Arthur felt dreadfully alone. As though he was deep underwater, at the bottom of the reservoir with his hands tied behind his back, or later, at the bottom of the mermaid fountain with the dreadful Amicus phantom dancing gleefully above him.

Without looking up, he knew that the boy was staring at him. Arthur could not resist and his eyes flickered up to meet the boy's.

He nearly screamed when he saw the face. The skin was as taught and grey as a mask, and it almost glistened in the flickering yellow light. And yet, he thought, unable to drag his eyes away, he seemed to recognise the features.

With a shock he realised where it was that he had seen it: the flyers on Mrs Farnham's floor. It was the face of the missing boy, Andrew Farnham.

Arthur got up, but the bus stopped suddenly and sent him hurtling on to the floor. When Arthur stood up, the

215

boy was exiting the bus, and the driver had closed the doors behind him.

'Wait!' Arthur cried. 'Wait!'

He ran down the aisle to the driver.

'Open the doors!' Arthur said.

'This your stop, is it?' the driver said cheerfully. 'Sorry about that!'

The doors opened and Arthur leaned out of the bus. He looked left and right, but there was no one there, only an empty country road surrounded by dark hills.

'Which direction did that boy go in?' Arthur asked the driver.

'Which boy?' the driver said.

'The one who just got off. He was wearing a hoodie,' Arthur said. 'We need to find him! He's the missing boy.'

'I'm sorry, son,' the bus driver chuckled. 'It's just been you and me on the bus this evening.'

'What?' Arthur said. 'No – he just got off.'

'I think I would have noticed,' the bus driver responded. 'I have to give everyone a ticket.'

'But why did you stop, then?' Arthur said. 'If there wasn't anyone to let on or off?'

'Have to,' the bus driver replied amicably. 'It's the rules.'

'It can't be right,' Arthur said. 'I saw him.'

The driver looked up at Arthur's tired, haunted face.

'Why don't you take a seat, lad?' he said. 'You look like you could do with a rest.'

Arthur meekly sat down and glanced outside as they drove off. The bus driver was right; there was no one there. Nothing but the cold, bleak landscape and Arthur's own tired reflection.

CHAPTER TWENTY

Chuk, Penny and Xanthe peered into the window of the art room, spying on Cornwall, who had been sitting at his desk, speaking anxiously on the phone for twenty minutes. Although they could not hear what he was saying, they could tell from the sweat on his upper lip that it was not good news.

Cornwall ended the call and threw his phone across the room, where it shattered against the wall. He put his face in his hands.

'Is he crying?' Penny asked.

'Looks like it,' Chuk replied grimly.

Cornwall shook himself, wiped away his tears with the back of his grubby sleeve and got up. He looked around the art block, checking that he was alone, and unlocked the cupboard behind him. He slid out a huge canvas,

218

swaddled in cloth, and began to move it towards the back door.

'What is that?' Chuk asked.

'We need to follow him,' Penny said.

They ran around the side of the art block and hid behind a tree as they watched Cornwall load the painting into the back of a van.

'He's going to get away!' Xanthe whispered.

'I've got an idea,' Chuk said. 'Xanthe, go and distract Cornwall. Penny, come with me.'

'Wait!' Xanthe hissed as Chuk and Penny ran off.

Xanthe took a deep breath and stepped out from behind the tree.

'Sir!' she called to Cornwall, who jumped at the sound of her voice.

He turned around and smiled at Xanthe calmly.

'Yes, Xanthe?' he said.

'Where are you going?' she asked.

'I'm just driving into Grimstone for some art supplies,' he replied.

'Oh, right.'

'Is there anything I can help you with, Xanthe?'

'I just wanted to ask you about our self-portraits,' Xanthe replied sweetly. 'Do you think they are any good?'

Cornwall looked at her suspiciously, weighing up his options. 'Yes,' he said slowly, 'they're all very good.'

'Great, I just wanted a high mark, that's all. I know we didn't get off on the right foot,' Xanthe continued, glancing behind her. What were Penny and Chuk doing?

'Don't worry,' Cornwall said. 'You'll all get very good marks.'

He opened the van door.

'Wait!' Xanthe said.

Cornwall paused.

'I . . . er . . . just wanted to ask you about . . . th-the Renaissance,' Xanthe stammered.

Cornwall's eyes narrowed. 'Xanthe,' he said quietly, walking towards her, 'what are you up to?'

'Nothing, sir!' she replied.

'Because if I didn't know any better, I'd think you were trying to stall me.'

'Why would I do that?' Xanthe laughed nervously.

Cornwall grabbed her by the arm. 'Who are you waiting for? Did you call one of the teachers?' he asked. He was panicking, she could see.

'No! I promise!' Xanthe squealed.

Cornwall searched her face. Xanthe winced.

'Right,' he growled. 'Get in the van.'

'No!' Xanthe tried to pull away.

'Get in!' he said, and shoved her into the passenger's seat.

He got in beside her and locked the door before she could get out.

'Don't worry,' he said as he put the key in the ignition. 'This won't take long.'

Chuk and Penny arrived as the van sped off. Chuk was driving an electric milk float, which the catering staff used to deliver food to the boarding houses. He'd swiped the keys from a hook in the kitchen.

'Where is Xanthe?' Penny asked.

'You don't think Cornwall . . . ?' Chuk replied.

'Go after the van,' Penny ordered. 'And turn your head-lights off – otherwise he'll see us.'

'OK,' Chuk said, uncertainly flicking a few switches on the dashboard.

'Step on it!' Penny shouted.

The van swung down the school drive ahead of them, skidding and weaving, sending dust flying into Penny and Chuk's eyes.

'What do we do if he leaves the grounds?' Chuk asked. 'We can't take this thing on the roads.'

'Oh, man up, Chuk,' Penny replied.

The van was slowing down near the gates.

'Shhh,' Penny said. 'He's pulling over.'

Chuk stopped the milk float and jumped out. 'Take it back to school and get someone who can help,' he said.

'I don't know how to drive it,' Penny replied.

'It's easy,' Chuk said, pointing at the pedals. 'Stop. Go.'

'But –'

'Hurry,' Chuk said, looking over at the van. 'I'll make sure Xanthe's OK.'

Penny didn't have time to argue. She slid over to the driver's seat and turned the cart around.

'Be careful,' she whispered.

Chuk darted behind a tree just as Cornwall got out of the van.

Cornwall had left his headlights on, illuminating the school gates and the misty road beyond.

Xanthe tried to open the van door but Cornwall kicked it shut.

'Shhhh. Calm down,' Cornwall said. 'We're just waiting for my friend.'

'What friend?' Xanthe said, dreading the answer.

'You'll see.'

Xanthe looked over to the driver's seat; the keys were swinging from the ignition. If only she knew how to drive.

Suddenly, a figure appeared in the headlights. Tall and white, it drifted out of the mist like an angel. An angel with black claws.

Xanthe hid behind the dashboard and held her breath.

'Strack . . .' Chuk whispered under his breath.

Helena Strack walked forward and gave Cornwall an icy peck on the cheek.

'Do you have it?' she asked.

'Y-y-yes,' Cornwall stammered. 'But . . . but . . . I've changed my mind. I told you last week, I don't want to do this. The figure in the painting . . . the Creeper . . . it's –'

Strack laughed, her breath hitting the cold air in plumes.

'Don't tell me you believe that ridiculous old story.'

'Give me more time,' he begged. 'I just need more time.'

'You've had plenty of time,' Strack snapped. 'Show it to me.'

Cornwall reluctantly walked to the back of the van and opened the doors.

'Bring it out into the light,' she ordered.

He slid the blanket-swaddled canvas out of the boot and carried it in front of the headlights.

Strack unwrapped the blanket and stood back, admiring the painting.

It was the Gainsborough from the library.

Chuk frowned. He had been in the library that afternoon and the painting had still been there. How had Cornwall found the time?

'And you're sure they don't know?' Strack asked, squinting at the paintwork.

'I swapped it for the copy a few weeks ago and hid the real one in a storeroom,' Cornwall said.

'How? It was hanging in the library, was it not?'

'One of the librarians is blind. I told her I was borrowing a few chairs.' Cornwall said.

'Clever boy,' Strack said. 'Well, I think that concludes our business. I'll take the van. You can walk back to Shiverton Hall.'

'There is just one tiny problem,' Cornwall said. Strack's smile faded. Cornwall nodded to the van.

Xanthe slid down lower but she knew she had been caught.

'What is this?' Strack hissed. 'What have you done?'

'She had told someone, I'm sure of it . . . they would have stopped me . . . you said you needed the painting tonight!' Cornwall whined.

Strack clutched his face with her black talons and made him look at her. 'And what do you think she'll tell people now?' she hissed. 'She's seen me. She's seen the painting. You really have lost it!'

Cornwall whimpered.

'Get out,' Strack said, opening the van door and pulling Xanthe out by her ponytail.

'Let me go,' Xanthe said.

'I'm afraid I can't,' Strack said. 'Because Mr Cornwall owes a very nasty man a lot of money, and if that nasty man doesn't get his money then we'll both be dead.'

'I won't tell anyone,' Xanthe whispered.

'I'm afraid I can't take that chance,' Strack sneered. She drew a long, thin blade from inside her coat. It glinted in the headlights.

'Don't,' Cornwall begged.

'Don't tell me what to do!' Strack screamed. 'This is your doing.'

'Sh-she isn't the only one who knows,' Cornwall stammered.

Strack turned on Cornwall. 'What do you mean?'

'There was a boy . . . Jake . . . He saw I'd hidden the painting in the storeroom.'

'Well, you'll just have to silence him, won't you?' Strack said.

'He's not here,' Cornwall said quietly. 'He didn't come back to school after half-term. He's in London.'

'Do I have to do everything?' Strack spat.

Strack turned to Xanthe and lifted the blade in the air.

Xanthe buried her head in her arms and waited for the sting of the knife.

But it did not come. She opened one eye and saw Strack swooning above her, a trickle of blood dripping on to her white dress. Strack dropped the knife and slumped forward, revealing Chuk behind her, holding a rock.

Cornwall sank to his knees, as the sound of sirens rippled in the distance.

CHAPTER TWENTY-ONE

The bus driver leaned forward. 'What's going on here?' he asked.

'What is it?' Arthur rushed to the front of the bus. The Shiverton gates seemed to be blocked by ambulances and police cars.

'Oh no,' Arthur whispered.

The bus doors opened and Arthur ran out to an astonishing sight. Xanthe was sitting in the back of an ambulance wrapped in a blanket. Cornwall had been handcuffed and was being forced into a police car, ranting and swearing. Penny and Chuk were talking to a police officer.

'What on earth has happened?' Arthur asked, rushing up to Xanthe. 'Are you OK?'

Xanthe smiled weakly. 'Never felt better,' she said. And then promptly fainted.

The police were taking photographs of the Gainsborough as Arthur walked over.

'Penny! Chuk!' Arthur called out urgently. 'Come and look at this.'

Penny and Chuk joined him by the painting.

'What is it?' Penny asked.

'Something's missing,' Arthur said.

'What?' Chuk asked, peering at the scene on the canvas.

'Oh no,' Penny whispered. 'The Creeper.'

Arthur marched over to Cornwall, who was sitting slumped in the back of the police car. 'How long has the real painting been hidden?' Arthur demanded.

Cornwall shrugged. 'A few weeks.'

'So you've let us think that our school was safe because the Creeper was still in the painting – only, it wasn't the real thing. You'd just painted it into your copy of the painting.'

'It's just a story,' Cornwall murmured.

'Yeah?' Arthur said. 'Then how do you explain the fact that the figure is missing from that picture over there?'

Cornwall glanced over at the painting. 'I'm so sorry,' he whispered.

Arthur, George and Penny sat in the Garnons library, discussing the madness of the past few hours while waiting for Toynbee to come and speak to them. Xanthe, meanwhile, had reluctantly gone to the sanatorium, at her housemistress's insistence.

'I cannot believe I missed it all,' George said, devastated.

'Count yourself lucky. Poor Xanthe nearly got stabbed to death,' Penny answered.

'So all along he just came here to steal the painting?' George said.

'Well, to be honest, he was hardly Teacher of the Year,' Arthur said. 'It's not that much of a shocker that he had an ulterior motive.'

'But, hang on, I thought Cornwall couldn't paint?' Penny said. 'How did he make a copy of the painting?'

Toynbee appeared, and sat wearily in an armchair by the fire.

'Good question, Penny,' Toynbee said. 'He's just confessed everything to the police. It turns out that Cornwall can not only paint, but is one of the world's most expert forgers. He was imprisoned for it until 1999, and then Strack found him and persuaded him to change his name, telling him she'd make him a star. He'd be rich and famous, as long as he made a few forgeries for her on the side. It seems to have been a rather lucrative business, until they sold one to the wrong man.'

'Who was it?'

'A rather frightening gentleman named Conrad Holst. He's cut off men's hands for less.'

'He was the man in the maze!' Arthur realised.

Toynbee nodded. 'He found out where Cornwall was,

and turned up here a couple of times to put the frighteners on him,' he said.

'No wonder Cornwall was so edgy,' Chuk said.

'I suppose the Gainsborough was irresistible.' Toynbee sighed. 'Worth a fortune, and far easier to steal from a school than a gallery filled with security guards. Cornwall coming to teach here gave him the time to paint the forgery. He and Strack planned to sell it to pay back Holst.'

'Strack!' Penny said with disgust. 'She's the worst of the lot. She was willing to kill Xanthe!'

'People will do almost anything when their lives are at risk,' Toynbee said quietly.

'How is Strack?' Chuk asked. 'I hit her pretty hard.'

'She'll be fine,' Toynbee replied. 'Or as fine as you can be in prison.'

'Best place for her,' George said.

Toynbee grimaced. 'Now I have to do the distasteful part,' he said. 'The powers that be have asked that you keep the details of this to yourselves for the time being. If anyone asks, the sirens were due to an accident on the road near the school gates.'

'What?' Chuk cried. 'That's ridiculous! If it hadn't been for us they would have got away with it! This deserves to be on the front page of *The Whisper*.'

'I have only told you what I myself have been asked,' Toynbee said. 'The school hopes to keep the matter out of the press at least until the end of term. Professor Long-Pitt does not want the students disrupted.'

Chuk shook his head angrily.

'Of course,' Toynbee continued, 'if someone *did* know the story, they would be a few days ahead of everyone else.'

He winked at Chuk.

'Sir,' Chuk said, 'are you suggesting it might be an idea for Penny and me to go to the *Whisper* offices?'

'I am saying nothing of the sort!' Toynbee said. 'But if I turn around to talk to Arthur and you two slip out, well, what can an old man do?'

Chuk grinned. 'Thank you, sir,' he said.

'For what?' Toynbee replied innocently, and turned to talk to Arthur.

Penny and Chuk took their cue, and slipped away from the room.

'I'm sorry I didn't believe you about Cornwall, Arthur,' Toynbee said.

'That's all right,' Arthur replied. 'Right now I'm more concerned about where the Creeper is.'

'That makes two of us,' Toynbee agreed grimly.

Arthur and George hurried towards Long-Pitt's study which had a dusty, old computer in the corner, the only computer in the whole school, and Long-Pitt's reluctant concession to the modern world.

'Are you sure this is a good idea?' George said nervously. 'Long-Pitt will string us up if she catches us.'

'At this point, I think Long-Pitt is the least of our worries,' Arthur said.

They reached the main school and sneaked down the dark corridors towards Long-Pitt's study.

Arthur opened the door and stepped in. 'I'll go,' he said. 'You stay out here and keep guard, and whistle if someone comes.'

'Not a flawless plan,' George said, as Arthur disappeared into the room.

The study was pitch black, but Arthur didn't want to draw attention to himself by turning the lights on. A stuffed crow, one of the room's many taxidermied creatures, glowered down at him from the rafters.

He hopped over Long-Pitt's desk to the computer and switched it on. It wheezed into life, booting up painfully slowly as the light of the monitor filled the room with a blue glow.

Arthur started typing. He had searched for the Creeper online while he was at home during half-term, but had come up with no more information than Cornwall had already told them. He combed through a few sites about monsters, hoping he might find something there. There were plenty: the Pale Man, the Slender Man, the Bunny Man, all internet legends, but not what Arthur was looking for.

He sat in front of the screen for a moment, his fingers poised hesitantly over the keyboard. He knew he had to do it.

He reluctantly typed it in.

SCRACCHENSHODDEREN

One result.

Arthur clicked on it.

The computer glitched, then the screen flickered up again. The website looked old and homemade. It was a single page – no links, no pictures.

It looked like a letter.

I'm sorry, it read.

If you are reading this, then I can't help you.

If you know his name, then you have called him. And he always answers.

I know I don't have long – I can feel him behind me. But I wanted to warn you.

This is my story.

My name is Liam. I am sixteen years old. I live in Oxford.

I was researching an essay in the Bodleian Library – my parents work at the university and so I have access to some of the old archive books. My essay was on a town called Grimstone and the witch-hunts that took place there in the eighteenth century. I'd found one book on the catalogue with the keywords 'Grimstone' and 'witch', an old diary from Grimstone. My mother dug it out for me from deep in the book stacks below Oxford, where it had sat untouched for years – she said it was so thick with dust that it took her ages to identify it.

The book itself was gobbledegook. I nearly didn't bother with it at all, but I changed my mind at the last minute and took it home.

I wish I hadn't. But I was fascinated by the middle page, and the weird word written on it:

Scracchenshodderen.

I should never have read that book. From the moment I did, I felt, well, you must know how I feel . . . Hunted. Watched.

I think I see him all the time, in reflections, in shadows, but when I look properly he's gone.

I first read that book two months ago, and every day that passes he is closer to me. Even standing in the sun I can feel his shadow on my back.

Sometimes I think others can see him too. A little girl on a train. My brother. But I'm never sure.

I know this sounds mad. I feel mad.

He thrives on fear. The more frightened I am, the closer he comes. He will try and scare you. He enjoys it. Try to keep him from your mind. You'll last longer.

Don't talk about him to anyone. There is a boy at school, my best friend, Alister. I showed him the book early on, before I fully understood what it meant. I can already see the grey-ness under his eyes, and the haunted look I know so well from my own reflection.

I cannot tell you what will happen to me. To us. But my hope is fading by the day. Kids go missing all the time. I don't know why I didn't think of them more before this. All those missing kids on the posters . . .

I'm almost looking forward to it. I don't want to think about him any more.

Good luck.

Liam,

October 2003

The website crashed before Arthur had the chance to reread it.

'Come on, come on!' Arthur murmured, clicking back to the original website. But the link was gone.

He typed *Alister and Liam Oxford* into the search engine. Hundreds of news websites appeared in the results.

LIAM REYNOLDS, 16, MISSING.

Arthur looked at the date. October. Maybe only a few days after Liam had written his warning.

A few weeks later were the next news stories.

SECOND BOY MISSING FROM OXFORD: ALISTER PARKER.

Arthur sat back in his chair, staring at the photograph of Liam Reynolds. Smiling. Happy. A little sunburned.

'What happened to you?' Arthur whispered.

Arthur realised he was shivering. The temperature in the study had plunged. He felt something move behind him, something brushing the hair on the nape of his neck.

Arthur wanted to call for George, but Liam's warning stilled his tongue.

A shape blinked on to the computer screen.

It was a hand. The hand he'd seen in the lake, and he was sure that it was the hand that had been tugging at his sleeve and tapping him softly on the back for the past few weeks.

The grey fingers unfurled, and then slowly they began to scratch at the screen. The sound made Arthur's whole body shudder, as though the long nails were scratching at his skin.

Arthur jumped up, desperate to get away, turning his back on the computer screen and the demonic hand.

He felt the bloodless fingers clasp his arm, catching him by the elbow.

'Get off!' Arthur shrieked, as the fingernails pierced through his shirt and tore at his skin.

'ARTHUR!'

Arthur spun around, blinking. The overhead light was on, and Long-Pitt was looming in the doorway, George standing behind her apologetically.

The monitor was black and silent, the hand nowhere to be seen.

'What on earth do you think are you doing in here?' Long-Pitt shouted.

'I-I . . .' Arthur said faintly. He didn't have the energy to argue with Long-Pitt.

'Count yourself lucky that it's nearly the end of term,' she said sharply. 'Otherwise I'd suspend you both.'

Arthur nodded.

'I realise that living without the internet can be trying for students with the attention span of gnats,' she sneered, 'but breaking into my office after lights-out is a serious infringement of the rules.'

'But it's an emergency!' George protested.

Long-Pitt raised her eyebrows.

'What kind of emergency?' she asked.

Arthur shook his head imploringly at a panicking George.

'Er . . .' George said, 'Nothing. Never mind.'

Long-Pitt studied the boys.

'You look pale, Arthur,' she said. 'Are you quite all right? I wouldn't want you perishing on my watch.'

'I'm fine,' Arthur replied tightly.

Long-Pitt narrowed her eyes.

'Well,' she said finally. 'Back to house with you both. Don't let me ever catch you out of bounds again!'

'Sorry, Professor,' they mumbled in unison.

'Some lookout you are,' Arthur whispered as they walked away.

'Hey!' George said. 'That woman is like a ghost. I didn't hear her until she was right behind me.'

'It's all right,' Arthur said. 'As it happens, I needed to get out of there anyway.'

'Did you find anything? About the Creeper?' George asked.

'Nothing new,' Arthur lied.

CHAPTER TWENTY-TWO

'What is up with you, Arthur?' Penny said, a week later. 'You look terrible.'

'I think it's just a bit of flu,' he replied.

She was right though. Arthur had been sleepless for so many nights he could barely keep his eyes open. Yet he didn't dare close them, because every time he did he saw the ghastly, grasping hand. He could hear the noise all the time now. *Scratch, scratch, scratch.* Even in broad daylight. It was getting louder by the day. *Scratch, scratch, scratch.* And all the time he went over what he knew in his head, but it didn't add up. Was *Scracchenshodderen* the name of the Creeper? He felt certain that it must be, that the two things were linked, but he had the nagging sensation that he was missing a crucial piece of the puzzle.

238

'Are you going to be all right on the CCF camping trip?' Penny asked. 'You look like you're about to keel over.'

'I'll be fine,' Arthur replied.

He didn't feel fine. Back in his room, he felt like death as he packed his camping gear.

Toynbee knocked on his door. 'May I step in?' he asked.

'Of course,' Arthur replied.

'Arthur, I hope you don't mind my saying, but you've been looking rather unwell this last week,' Toynbee said.

'I don't feel that well either,' Arthur sighed.

'Is something the matter?'

'I think something is after me.'

'What do you mean, *something*?' Toynbee asked.

Arthur stayed silent.

'Arthur,' Toynbee said gently, 'whatever it is, you must tell me.'

'I can't,' Arthur whispered.

'I won't leave until I have it out of you.' Toynbee sighed. 'If I have to suspend you, I will.'

Arthur took a deep breath. 'All right,' he said, 'but don't say I didn't warn you.'

After Arthur had detailed Liam's letter, Toynbee sat and thought for a minute.

'It is peculiar,' Toynbee conceded. 'Perhaps this creature, this *Scracchenshodderen*, possesses objects. That might explain why it was in the book and the painting.'

'I hadn't thought of that,' Arthur said.

'There are stories of object possession,' Toynbee said, 'but I have never encountered it myself. It is highly unusual. But a creature that inhabits two different objects – unheard of!'

Toynbee cleaned his glasses on his cardigan, obviously thinking hard.

'Well, the first thing is,' he said finally, 'you'd better stop packing for the CCF trip. The last place you should be right now is in the Grimstone woods.'

Arthur looked crestfallen.

'Surely it'd be better than being here by myself? Everyone in my year will be there,' Arthur said.

'It would be better for me to keep an eye on you here,' Toynbee said.

'I guess,' Arthur said, 'It's just . . .'

'Just what?'

'I was really looking forward to it,' Arthur replied quietly. 'The whole year is going.'

Toynbee considered this.

'I don't want to keep you from your friends, Arthur.'

Arthur looked up at his housemaster hopefully. 'Does that mean I can go?' he asked. 'Do you think it's safe?'

'I wish I knew,' Toynbee replied, 'but I don't know that the school will be any safer.'

Arthur nodded.

'You can go,' Toynbee said hesitantly, 'but you must

promise me to stay in sight of someone at all times. And I'll give you your mobile back from the lock-up, just in case. I know Long-Pitt hates them but I think you'll agree that this is an extenuating circumstance.'

'Yes!' Arthur said. 'Thank you, sir.'

Toynbee sighed. 'Promise me you'll be careful?'

'I'll do my best,' Arthur said.

The Grimstone woods were freezing as the CCF squadron struggled to put up their army-issue tents. It took Penny almost an hour, during which she threatened to throw it on the campfire at least three times.

'Honestly, Penny,' George said. 'Even I managed it.'

'Shut up, George,' Penny sighed.

'Managed to get a story published in a national newspaper but doesn't know how to follow simple instructions.' George tutted.

Earlier that week Chuk had sent a copy of *The Whisper* to his father, and he had run the story of Cornwall and Strack's fall from grace on the front page, crediting Chuk, Penny and Xanthe and offering them all summer jobs at his most prestigious title, *The Daily Journal*. George had been teasing Penny about it as much as he could 'to keep her feet on the ground'.

'Come on,' Arthur said to Penny, 'I'll help you.'

Soon they were all sitting around the campfire, giggling and toasting marshmallows. Even the Forge triplets had relaxed a bit, and were busy painting commando stripes on themselves with mud.

Arthur closed his eyes and felt the warmth of the fire on his face, but nothing could quite warm the cold in his blood.

Arthur lay awake in their tent, listening to the rustlings and hootings of the woods. They'd spent the evening around the campfire, laughing and telling stories, and had all gone to bed late. Arthur felt sure he was the only person awake. George was snoring next to him, and he could hear Xanthe mumbling in her sleep a few metres away.

The moonlight cast the shadow of the trees over the thin fabric of the tent. He buried his head in his sleeping bag and tried not to think about what might be outside.

A fingernail on nylon makes a very distinctive sound, a nauseating, snagging scrape. It was not the sound that Arthur wanted to hear coming from the outside of his tent in the middle of the night.

He peered out from beneath his sleeping bag.

He could see the shadow of a hand with long, tapered fingers. It was slowly circling the tent, running a sharp talon across the fabric as it did so, brushing it, stroking it, then . . . ripping it.

Arthur reached inside his sleeping bag for his phone: no reception. He sat up, careful not to wake George. He was paralysed with indecision. If he shouted, would he put the others in danger? He couldn't be sure.

He thought it over. If he ran as fast as he could, he might make Grimstone high street in five minutes. There was a phone box there. He could call Toynbee, and maybe the creature wouldn't follow him out of the woods.

The scratching began again.

Arthur couldn't think straight, his mind was addled with exhaustion and fear. All he knew was he had an overwhelming urge to run.

Arthur unzipped his sleeping bag, tooth by tooth, praying that the creature would not hear him. When he saw that the shadow was at the head of the tent, Arthur ripped open the flap and bolted towards Grimstone.

The woods were silent as Arthur rushed through them, stones tearing at the soles of his feet and branches striking his face. He could hardly breathe with terror, but he ran on, holding his phone ahead of him to provide some light.

Suddenly he could hear the faint sound of footsteps running behind him, but he didn't dare turn back and slow himself down. It sounded like two sets of footsteps at least, but he couldn't be sure. And was that someone calling his name? He could barely hear anything over the sound of his heart pounding and his laboured breathing. The mobile slipped from his sweaty grip and fell to the ground. Arthur hesitated for a moment, then ran on: he didn't dare stop to pick it up.

He could feel the distance closing, and, seizing his chance, Arthur swerved suddenly and sharply to the left. The footsteps seemed to stumble. Arthur swerved again, and he heard the footsteps falter and stop. Was he alone? Had he done it?

He saw a light in the distance through the trees, and ran towards it. He didn't care what it was. Light meant people, and if he could get there he might have a chance. The trees cleared and when he saw where the light was coming from he nearly sobbed with relief.

It was Rose Cottage.

He sprinted down the path and hammered at the door.

'Who is it?' Mrs Todd's voice called through the door. 'I'll call the police.'

'It's Arthur,' Arthur said, trying to keep his voice down, conscious that at any moment he might be caught. 'Please let me in.'

Mrs Todd opened the door and Arthur nearly knocked her over in his haste to get inside.

'Lock the door,' Arthur panted. 'Please.'

Mrs Todd did so.

'What on earth are you doing here, Arthur?' Mrs Todd asked. 'It's nearly two o'clock in the morning!'

'Please,' Arthur gasped. 'Call Doctor Toynbee.'

'Doctor Toynbee?' Mrs Todd asked. 'Why?'

'Please,' Arthur repeated. 'I'll explain everything later on.'

Mrs Todd went into the other room. He heard her speaking on the telephone. 'Yes,' he heard her say. 'Arthur . . . I don't know . . . he insisted you come right away.'

Arthur sank down on to the sofa as Mrs Todd returned.

'He's on his way,' she said. 'What on earth has happened?'

Arthur explained, as briefly as he could, the extraordinary circumstances that had brought him to her door. Mrs Todd listened with astonishment. When he had finished, she took a deep breath.

'It sounds as though you're in trouble, Arthur,' she said, apprehensively. 'Once Scracchenshodderen has your scent, there is little any of us can do.'

Arthur felt his heart falter.

He had not mentioned that name.

In fact, he had taken great care not to.

'When will Toynbee be here?' Arthur asked with a calmness he didn't feel.

'Soon,' Mrs Todd replied.

He studied Mrs Todd. Why had she been awake and dressed at two in the morning? Her hands were folded in her lap; he had never really noticed them before, but they were skeletal, long-fingered and there was dust between the blue ridges of her veins.

How old was she?

Arthur felt the panic clutch at him.

'I'm lucky you were up,' Arthur said steadily. 'Why are you awake so late?'

'I'm waiting for my children,' Mrs Todd replied, with a smile.

'Your children?' Arthur asked hoarsely.

'Yes,' she said. 'I think you may know them.'

Arthur stood up.

'Don't bother, Arthur,' Mrs Todd said. 'You're locked in. And even if you weren't, I have plenty of ways to make you stay.'

'Who are you?' Arthur said.

'Who am I?' she laughed. 'That's a good question, Arthur Shiverton.'

Arthur felt like he might be sick. 'How did you know?' he asked faintly.

'I knew the moment you arrived last term.' She sniffed the air. 'The Shiverton blood is quite . . . pungent, you know.'

'Let me go, please,' Arthur begged.

'Ha!' Mrs Todd spat. 'I'm sure those were the very words my daughter used before your ancestor murdered her.'

'Daughter . . . ?' Arthur repeated, all the stories that George had told him suddenly rushing back to him. He looked at Mrs Todd with horror.

'There it is!' Mrs Todd laughed.

'Rose Cottage,' Arthur whispered. For the first time he

noticed the pink, velvet ribbon, tied in a bow around a candlestick on the mantelpiece.

'Named after my dear, departed daughter,' Mrs Todd replied.

'But how can you . . . ? That was centuries ago,' Arthur said.

'And I am centuries older than that still,' Mrs Todd said.

'Mrs Todd,' Arthur began.

'Arthur, come now,' she said coyly. 'I think we know each other well enough that you can call me by my real name.'

'Ma Watkins,' Arthur whispered.

'Oh, that was one of my names, certainly. But not my first,' she said. 'Ma was short for Mary. My first name was Mary. Although I was known for some time as Grey Mary.'

Arthur shook his head. 'It's impossible!' he said.

'Is it?' she replied. 'I would have thought that you of all people would no longer question the impossible.'

'How did nobody notice you?' Arthur asked.

'No one ever notices a sweet, old lady. A few name changes, a few lies . . . Dear old Mrs Todd had to go, of course, so that I could borrow her house. I knew how to blend in – unlike my sister.'

'Your sister?' Arthur asked.

'Ann,' Ma Watkins replied. 'She couldn't resist showing off, though I begged her not to.'

247

'The witch in the well,' Arthur said. 'The poisoner.'

'Indeed. She took after our poor mother. Mother was burned at the stake. The smell of burning still hangs around me to this day.'

For the first time, Arthur noticed the cloying perfume, which didn't wholly mask the stench of burning hair.

'I'm sorry they burned your mother,' Arthur said carefully.

'Are you?' Ma Watkins laughed. 'You wouldn't be sorry if you'd known her. She would have plucked out your eyes and swallowed them whole.'

'Toynbee will be here soon,' Arthur said.

Ma Watkins shouted with laughter, revealing rows of rotting teeth. Her appearance was becoming more repulsive by the minute. Her orange wig had slipped to one side, revealing a bald, scabbed scalp.

'You are rather slow, Arthur Shiverton, like the rest of your accursed line. Do you really think that I would call Toynbee here?'

Arthur slumped down on to the sofa. 'What do you want from me?' he asked.

'I don't want anything from you. Although, my son may feel differently,' she said slyly.

'Your son? But I thought Rose was your only –'

'She was my only blood child, yes. But I have had many children, stolen from the village in the night.' Ma Watkins listed them on her bony hands: 'Dear Zezia and Violetta

248

and Malvolio and Skinless Tom, and of course, the two who became Husband and Wife. There were others, too, who didn't last so long.'

Arthur struggled to understand what she was saying.

'The stories . . .' he said. 'The stories you've been telling me are about the children that Grey Mary took?'

'My children!' Ma Watkins shouted, her pupils dilating into angry points. 'My own family was taken from me.'

She steadied herself, taking a deep breath.

'Everyone deserves a family, Arthur,' she said. 'Unfortunately, human children die awfully easily, as you are soon to find out.'

Arthur cast around the room for anything he might be able to use as a weapon, while Ma Watkins began to tell the story of her children.

'I realised that if I wanted my family to stay with me, I needed to find some way to free them from their human bodies. It was a very complicated procedure, some of the greatest magic this country has ever seen.'

'How did you do it?' Arthur said, hoping to buy himself some time. There was a poker by the fire, if he could only . . .

'I freed them from their bodily form, and gave each child an object to possess. Something they could hibernate in, if you will. They had to be attractive objects, items that people would covet. Zezia had her typewriter; poor Tom, who lost his skin, had a mirror; Husband and Wife had their cane filled with dice; and my circus children used those marvellous magic boxes.'

Suddenly, Arthur noticed the dusty typewriter on Ma Watkins's desk and the enamelled hand-mirror on her side table . . . and the poker leaning up against the fireplace was not a poker at all, but a walking cane with a pewter top.

'They use the objects to possess people,' Arthur said, dragging his eyes away from the typewriter.

'That was the darkest magic of all, a very complicated spell indeed, a spell that let them pass into the bodies of others.'

'Where are they now?' Arthur whispered.

'The human spirit is a delicate thing,' Ma Watkins said bitterly. 'Many of my children became restless, and tired of their constant search for bodies. They begged me to free them from their purgatory.'

'And did you?' Arthur asked.

'I am their mother,' Ma Watkins snapped. 'I would do anything for my children. The ones who asked were freed. Only two remain. My most beloved children. The twins.'

'The twins . . .' Arthur repeated faintly.

'Do you think you can guess who they might be?' Ma Watkins asked with a twisted smile.

'The Creeper . . .' Arthur realised.

'Finally,' Ma Watkins said, 'you get something right. The first is the Creeper, although I always called him Farrus.'

Arthur heard a creak from the floorboards above them.

Ma Watkins looked up. 'Ah,' she said, 'we've woken him.'

Arthur heard footsteps on the stairs.

A shadow appeared in the doorway.

'Come in, my dear,' Ma Watkins said.

When Arthur saw who it was, he wanted to scream.

'Jake!' Arthur cried, jumping up. 'What's going on?'

Ma Watkins laughed. 'That isn't Jake,' she said. 'That is Farrus.'

'But Jake's at home. He's in London,' Arthur whispered.

'Is he?' Ma Watkins asked. 'I must say it's astonishing that all it took was a letter stating that Jake was staying at home until the end of the term. Handwriting is so easy to forge. But you would have thought that the school might have checked it out a bit more – given their appalling safety record.'

'Jake,' Arthur said, shaking his friend. 'Are you all right?'

Jake grabbed Arthur's hands, with more force than Arthur had thought humanly possible, and threw him back on to the sofa.

'Jake isn't here,' Jake said, in a flat, strange voice.

There was a scratch at the door.

'Oh, goody!' Ma Watkins said. 'Now the fun really starts!'

251

'Who is that?' Arthur said.

'That is Farrus's twin. Dear, pale Peter. A strange boy. He has always been my favourite.'

'Peter?'

Ma Watkins laughed. 'You have come to know him rather well these past few weeks, I think, or at least, he has come to know you.'

'Scracchenshodderen,' Arthur whispered.

'He has so enjoyed watching you,' Ma Watkins said, as the scratching grew louder.

'And do you know why I love Peter so? Even more than my other children?' She sang.

'Why?' Arthur asked, already dreading the answer.

'Because Peter was always the cleverest. He didn't bother himself with bodies. Bodies rot. No, Peter chose something else.'

'What?' Arthur whispered.

'Why, souls, of course!' Ma Watkins cried gleefully. 'He gathers the souls of children. Pure, sweet souls never fester or perish. Only Peter saw that.'

'Yeah,' Arthur said, 'well, not for long!'

He reached back and pulled something out of his pyjama pocket.

'What are you doing?' Ma Watkins asked.

Arthur brought out the burned book. 'This is his object, right?' he said, waving it at Ma Watkins.

Ma Watkins smiled.

Arthur walked over to the fire. 'I'll throw it in,' Arthur said, holding the book over the flames.

'Be my guest,' Ma Watkins said.

Arthur called her bluff and tossed the book on the fire.

Ma Watkins sighed and walked over to the fire, plucking the book from the flames, unharmed except for a smudge of ash.

'Thank you for giving it back,' she said, sweetly, and slotted it on to her bookshelf. 'It's not the book, you silly boy, it's the name.'

Arthur watched in despair.

The scratching on the door grew louder.

'I think we'd better let him in, don't you?' Ma Watkins asked.

The door flew open.

At first, Arthur could not see its face. The creature was so tall that the doorway could not accommodate it, and all Arthur could see was its bone-thin, ragged body. Its long, lily-white fingers curled around the doorframe and it hauled itself into the cottage.

Arthur looked at the face and felt the bile burning up his throat. Scracchenshodderen had no features, just a smooth, grey, glistening blank where a face should be.

'Hello, my dear,' Ma Watkins said.

'I . . . I don't understand,' Arthur stammered. 'He had a different face . . .'

Ma Watkins cackled. 'Do you mean this one?'

The skin on Scracchenshodderen's face began to distort and stretch, and features began to wriggle their way out of it, like a chick pushing its way out of an egg.

Soon Andrew's face stared back at him, and then the face distorted again and Liam's face appeared, churning out of the grey. The face mutated many times; some of the faces Arthur recognised, most of them he didn't. Andrew's face reappeared.

'We're all in here, Arthur,' the creature said, a dozen voices speaking at once – all of the boys that Scracchenshodderen had hunted. 'You'll be joining us soon.'

'No!' Arthur cried.

'You'll enjoy it,' the voices hissed.

'There's a good boy,' Ma Watkins said.

'All right,' Arthur said. 'I won't struggle. I won't even scream. Please just let Jake go.'

Farrus looked at Ma Watkins. 'But I like this body,' he said petulantly.

'Please,' Arthur begged. 'Think of Rose and how terrible it was when Lord Shiverton took her.'

'Shut up!' Ma Watkins said.

'Jake's mother will miss him just as much as you miss her,' he pleaded. 'It's me you want. Please, leave Jake out of it.'

Ma Watkins thought for a moment.

'Why not?' she said finally.

Farrus stamped his foot.

'We don't need that sickly boy,' Ma Watkins said, dismissively gesturing to Jake's thin body. 'Join your brother. Shiverton blood will taste much better.'

Arthur watched as Scracchenshodderen gripped Farrus with his long fingers. Jake's body began to shudder, and Farrus began to scream. After about a minute, a new face pushed itself out of Scracchenshodderen's grey skin, and Jake fell back, landing in an unconscious heap on the floor.

'Well,' Ma Watkins said, 'a deal's a deal.'

Scracchenshodderen stood over Arthur and smiled. Arthur felt an agony like nothing he had ever experienced. It felt as though his blood was being sucked, cell by cell, out of every pore.

Arthur knew he must do something.

'You say you steal souls?' Arthur yelled. 'Pure souls, children's souls? Well why would you want mine? Mine isn't pure.'

'Don't listen to him,' Ma Watkins shouted.

Arthur closed his eyes and thought about the day by the reservoir. He thought about the time he attacked the bullies, the feeling of power, and of fury, and the hot blood on his hands.

He could feel Scracchenshodderen pull back, confused.

Arthur thought about the burned man and the way he had threatened Arthur's family, and the way that Helena Strack had nearly killed Xanthe to get her hands on the painting. He thought about everything that had ever made him angry, the Forge triplets, Long-Pitt, Cornwall. Suddenly he felt his skin burning.

'What's going on?' Ma Watkins screamed at her son. 'Why haven't you taken him?'

Scracchenshodderen staggered back and let go of Arthur.

'Get him!' Ma Watkins said.

Scracchenshodderen shook his head.

'Well, if you won't do it, then I'll have to,' Ma Watkins hissed. Arthur watched as the body of Mrs Todd fell to the floor, and Ma Watkins's repulsive features appeared in Scracchenshodderen's face. Her face was barely human at all, no more than a huge gaping mouth filled with rows of pointed teeth. The hands gripped Arthur and lifted him off the ground.

'I'm going to enjoy this,' Ma Watkins hissed.

'Wait!' Arthur said.

Scracchenshodderen paused.

'What?' Ma Watkins shouted.

'This isn't a fair fight,' Arthur said, a plan crystallising in his mind.

'Who said anything about fair?' Ma Watkins's gaping mouth screamed, as Scracchenshodderen's grip tightened around him.

'You say you're the most powerful witch in the country,' Arthur said, 'so prove it. Pit yourself against me in a fair fight, and we'll see who wins.'

Arthur grabbed Husband and Wife's walking stick from the fireplace. 'How about a game of dice?' he asked.

Ma Watkins laughed, a screeching laugh that rippled through the house.

'A game, then, Arthur Shiverton,' she said. 'A *fair* fight.'

Arthur screwed his eyes shut, and shook the cane. The dice began to rattle.

Ma Watkins continued to laugh her sputtering, hideous laugh.

'You fool, Arthur!' she said as the dice tumbled over one another. 'The dice are fixed. As in life, evil always wins.'

The dice stopped. Arthur looked down.

'The moon,' he said. 'Death.'

'Just as I thought,' Ma Watkins said, stepping towards Arthur once more.

'Wait!' Arthur said.

Ma Watkins paused.

'I didn't say whose death,' Arthur said.

'I know whose death! Yours!' Ma Watkins screeched.

Arthur smiled and tipped the cane towards Ma Watkins so that she could see.

'A dagger,' Ma Watkins said disbelievingly. 'It's not possible.'

'The enemy,' Arthur said. 'I think that means you.'

Scracchenshodderen's body began to shake.

'No!' Ma Watkins roared. 'I made those dice myself! It can't be! Evil must win . . . It always wins.'

257

'I would have thought that you would know better,' Arthur said, feeling his blood boiling in his veins, 'than to play a Shiverton in a game of evil.'

The scream that emitted from the creature was so loud that it shattered the windows of Rose Cottage. It began to shake. Arthur could see the lungs struggling behind the grey ribs. It clawed at its throat, choking.

'No,' Ma Watkins wheezed. 'No!'

It staggered about, gasping for air, and then made one final grab for Arthur, with its sharp talons, pulling him close to its stinking, cavernous mouth. 'I'll get you, Arthur Shiverton,' it hissed in Ma Watkin's dry cackle. 'We've only just begun.'

'Good luck with that,' Arthur sneered, and pushed it away. The creature gurgled and thrashed about, spraying Arthur with oleaginous, grey blood. It shuddered and, with a final gurgling cry, exploded, coating the room, and Arthur, in a hot, foul-smelling oil.

Arthur waited, stunned. He felt a stirring in the room beside him, and Jake sat up blearily, rubbing the sticky mess from his glasses.

'What happened?' Jake asked. 'Where are we?'

There was another knock on the door.

'Arthur!' a voice yelled from outside. 'Let us in!'

Arthur had never been more relieved to see the Forge triplets.

CHAPTER TWENTY-THREE

A rthur had lost count of the number of times Toynbee had apologised.

'You can leave early,' Toynbee said. 'I'd understand if you want to go home.'

Arthur shook his head. 'There's no need, sir.' Arthur grinned. 'Now that Ma Watkins is gone, the school is safe.'

'Let us hope that is the case,' Toynbee said. 'Are you sure you're all right, Arthur?'

'Yes, sir,' Arthur said. 'It's just . . .'

'What?'

'Well, that fortune teller in the magic shop, Alan, he told me that he saw something terrible in my future,' Arthur said.

'Well, it seems that he was right,' Toynbee said. 'You

don't get more terrible than what happened to you last night.'

'No,' Arthur agreed. 'But he said that I was going to do something terrible.'

Toynbee frowned. 'Arthur, you mustn't feel guilty about what you did last night. It was necessary. They would have killed you.'

'I know, sir,' Arthur said. 'But I don't think that was what Alan meant. Something happened, while the Scracchenshodderen was trying to take me. I think he saw something too. It made him want to stop, to leave me alone.'

'Arthur, we have had this conversation before. Just because you are a Shiverton, that does not mean there is something wrong with you.'

'It only means that, in a game of dice, I am more evil than the darkest witch in the world.'

Toynbee did not reply.

'I'd better get to Long-Pitt's class,' Arthur sighed. 'There are no excuses for being late for her class. Even nearly being murdered by an ancient monster.'

On his way to Long-Pitt's lesson, Arthur spotted the Forge triplets across the quad, and ran to thank them for coming to find him the night before.

'Dan!' Arthur called, but the triplets did not seem to hear him. 'Oi, guys!'

Arthur reached them, and the triplets stopped.

'I just wanted to say thank you,' Arthur said, panting.

Dan frowned and looked around in an exaggerated way. 'Can you hear anything, boys?' he said. 'I thought I just heard something.'

The other triplets sniggered and shook their heads.

'Must have just been the wind,' Dan said, looking straight into Arthur's eyes.

'What are you doing?' Arthur said suspiciously.

'Nothing at all, Scholarship,' Dan said, cracking his knuckles. 'Let's just say our incentive to be nice to you no longer applies, so we can begin where we left off last term. Namely, with us hating your guts.'

'What do you mean, *incentive?*' Arthur asked.

Dan tapped his nose. 'I'd say that's none of your business,' he sneered.

'Long-Pitt made us,' one of Dan's brothers said. 'She said we'd have straight As all term if we kept an eye on you. She seems to think we failed last night, so we've been relieved of our duties.'

'What?' Arthur asked.

Dan hit his brother on the side of the head. 'Shut up, you imbecile,' he hissed.

'But Long-Pitt hates me,' Arthur said, baffled.

'Yeah, and so do we,' Dan scoffed. 'But everyone's got their price, don't they?'

*

261

Arthur watched Long-Pitt as she outlined Oscar Wilde's main themes on the blackboard, his mind racing.

Penny was sitting beside Arthur and had been frantically writing him notes all through class; he already had about six pieces of paper in his pencil case scrawled in Penny's writing with: *WHERE WERE YOU LAST NIGHT???* and *WHAT HAPPENED???* Arthur thought that it was probably too complicated a story to write in a note.

At the end of the lesson, as the students gathered their things, Arthur approached Long-Pitt's desk.

'Can I talk to you for a minute, Professor?' he asked. 'It's very important.'

Long-Pitt waited for the last student to file out, and then looked up impatiently at Arthur.

'Yes?' she said.

'Did you bribe the Forge triplets to look after me this term?' Arthur asked.

Long-Pitt's cool demeanour was momentarily comprom-ised. 'I don't know what you're talking about,' she said finally.

'No?' Arthur said. 'And it's just a coincidence that you happened to be in the woods all those times that I was there too, is it?'

Long-Pitt remained silent, but her expression dared Arthur to go on.

'Why?' Arthur asked. 'You don't even like me!'

'You flatter yourself that I have any opinion of you whatsoever,' Long-Pitt replied.

'OK, fine,' he said. 'But after what happened last night I think I at least deserve to know what's been going on round here.'

Long-Pitt sighed. 'At the beginning of this term, I was contacted by someone who quite forcefully impressed upon me the importance of keeping you out of harm's way.'

'Who?'

Long-Pitt smiled.

'*Who?*' Arthur repeated.

'Your father,' Long-Pitt said finally.

Arthur frowned.

'What do you mean?' he said. 'That can't be right. My father is dead.'

Long-Pitt raised her eyebrows. 'He didn't look dead to me,' she said.

Arthur groped the desk behind to steady himself.

'You've met him, I believe. You'd remember; he is rather distinctive-looking.'

'The burned man,' Arthur whispered.

'Indeed. Not a pretty face, but then, it is a miracle he survived the accident at all.'

'I don't . . .' Arthur stammered. 'Why didn't he tell me?'

'I'm sure he felt it would be . . . confusing for you if you knew.'

'So he scared me half to death instead?'

'In order to try and keep you safe,' Long-Pitt corrected. 'Once he realised that you were determined to come back to Shiverton Hall, he asked me to meet him in London. He felt it was too dangerous, being a male Shiverton, to come here himself.'

'But I saw him,' Arthur said, suddenly realising. 'On the hill, when we were doing CCF volunteering.'

'I believe he did come once, yes. Quite a risk for him to come to this place. It's not all that safe for one of Lord Shiverton's descendents, as I'm sure you'll have noticed.'

'Where is he now?' Arthur asked.

'I haven't the faintest idea,' Long-Pitt said coldly. 'Will that be all?'

'Yes,' Arthur said. 'That'll be all.'

Arthur walked out on to the quad with hesitant steps. It was warm, spring was finally beginning, and his friends were taking their break on the lawn, in a longed-for patch of sunlight. Penny spotted Arthur and waved him over, but Arthur found himself faltering. The sunlight hurt his eyes and the thought of joining his classmates filled him with a sudden intense revulsion.

It was happening again – the poisonous thoughts, the hotness in his blood, the flash of anger like a capillary bursting. But this time he didn't resist; he let it flood through him, feeling it lap at every corner of his body.

It felt good.

Without a glance back at his friends, he retreated into the darkness of Shiverton Hall.

EMERALD FENNELL is a writer and actress. She started writing scary stories when she was a child – much to the horror of some of her teachers. She studied English Literature at Oxford University but chose to spend most of her time reading spooky tales of terror. Emerald likes to write the Shiverton Hall books in the middle of the night.